Disclaimer

The story you are about to read is based on true
events. Names have been changed to protect all rights
and privacy.

Table of Content

Acknowledgments

There are 3 main components of man which are physical, mental and spiritual. Although all 3 of these come from Allah, it is my belief that the spiritual essence of man is what has eternal life. I believe this part of man is where God breathed into us to give us life. His breath of life was in me and with me the whole time I was in prison enduring. He was always there guiding me, helping me and sending people to help me. I first and foremost wish to thank Almighty Allah for everything He has done for me. He granted me my life and my freedom for what I believe is a divine purpose. Each day He allows me to remain alive is another opportunity to do something good for my spirit fighting in His cause to which I am eternally grateful in my belief.

I would like to thank my mother Mrs. Teresa Moore for dedicating her life to being not only the best mother any child could hope for, but for striving hard all of her life trying to be the type of person who is pleasing to God. Thank you mama for supporting me for 27 years even while you were weakened with a broken heart. I thank you mama for being on the other end of that phone call on the day I found out I was coming home. I thank you for believing in me. My love for you is eternal. This book is dedicated to you.

I would like to thank my Godmother Ms. Alvira Henry. I know you are watching over me. You were a second mother to me and stood by my side trying to facilitate my release from prison. No words can be used to thank you enough. This book is dedicated to you.

To my brother Ralph. There is no me without you. You fought hard for me and made many sacrifices. You taught me unconditional love. You taught me how to be more patient

3

even when I thought I was being patient enough. You came and supported me at every prison, every parole hearing and never complained. You listened and you believed in me enough to make the necessary sacrifices. You nearly gave up everything so I would someday be free and I am so thankful to have a big brother like you. You are smart, kind, loving, amazing, charismatic, and inspiring. I also dedicate this book to you.

To my beloved Tracy who is no longer with me but who I hold near and dear in my heart. Tracy, you never stopped believing in me and never lost hope right up to the day God called you back to Him. I am so honored to have shared time with you on this earth. My love for you is eternal.

To my sister Janice Moore. You promised me that you would stand by me. You certainly did keep that promise. You risked your own life driving through inclement weather to visit me so I wouldn't feel alone or forsaken. That means more to me than anything.

My friend (my brother) Salih, what can I say. You are the example that was sent to me as a beacon in life. You believed in me like no other man has beside my brother Ralph. I was blessed to have you in my life as a spiritual brother in faith and as a best friend. The values you taught me are a part of me. You have taught me so much about life. It is truly indeed an honor and blessing for me to have been blessed to learn from such an honorable man.

To my brother Willie (Taq) Triplett for putting up with me and supporting me. You made sure that we had what we needed when we were going through our trying times. I thank you for the opportunities that you have provided me in life, because with you I have my freedom.

To Imam Wali Al-Amin (Willie Triplett Sr.) for being our voice in the prison when we had none. Thank you for making sure that the system did not mistreat us. You sacrificed your private life to come into the prison and teach us and fight for our right to practice our religion. You were more than just an Imam teaching us religion in the prison. You became a father image for many of us.

Special Acknowledgments

To Johnny Cochran who is no longer with us for giving me great insight, patience, passion and a better understanding, of the law.

Attorneys Gary and Janise Margosina.
Senator Carl Levin.
Mr. William Davidson of the Justice Department.
Doctor Chris Kay, eye surgeon.

Ty'rome Moore (nephew) who is my rock. You were 6 years old when I went to prison and you became part of my motivation to fight hard for my freedom. You stuck my me throughout my time in prison and I am so grateful.

Doctor Brian Lee, thank you for your brilliance in eye surgery. Nurse Carol Bennett, I thank you for courageously doing everything in your power to override the prison officials and helping save my life. I am eternally grateful. There were so many who stood by me who I have not mentioned and I wish to thank them all.

Very Special Acknowledgment

To my brother (writer) and confidant, the **multi-talented,** Clark Triplett. It is taught by Allah that all things concerning our sojourn on earth are already written. Our

Creator gives all of us special gifts. My dear brother Clark, it was already written in the record of life held by our Lord that you would be the one who would be best suited to tell my story to the world. You have been given the gift of writing whether it be books, movie scripts, poetry or music. You wanted to remain humble and did not want to be acknowledged in this book for those gifts bestowed and for your vision, your creativity, your education, your dedication, your devotion, determination, discipline, beliefs, heart, body, soul, (blood, sweat, and tears), and let's not forget your loyalty unto this book project I asked you to take on.

I chose to do this special acknowledgment because my dear brother, you truly deserve it. I am sure you will debate with me that it was not you but rather me who made all of this happen by God's will. You are too modest. None of this could have happened without you and your talent and abilities and your unselfish sacrifices. I assure you my friend that you have taught me so much. You opened your home, to me and my wife and shared your family with us after we moved to Atlanta. You made writing this book greater than just an adventure. You made it become an amazing journey. I look forward to you writing the next chapter in my life. Thanks brother. I love you much.

Chapter 1
My Humbled Beginning

You know, everybody is always praying for a miracle. No matter what the struggle, every one of us has begged for or hoped for some kind of divine intervention in the form of a great miracle to help us out of tough situations, whether it be for health, money or some situation with the law. I know I've had my share. I actually had one of the greatest miracles imaginable happen to me and if I hadn't experienced it myself, if someone had told me my story, I would have probably thought, this is just too unbelievable. Well, the fact I am alive telling you my story is proof miracles do happen. I am Maurice Moore and I would like to share with you my story so that you can know and believe that miracles do happen.

Now before I tell you about the great miracle that happened to me, I would like to tell you a little bit about myself to help you understand how some of my past experiences led to my need for a divine miracle. I was born in Cleveland Ohio. I grew up in the small town of Flint, Michigan which is about 60 miles north of Detroit. Flint was made famous for being the birthplace of Buick cars and more recently for it's water crisis which became world wide news. My family moved there when I was 6 years old. I was the youngest of 6 children so I was kinda spoiled. We lived on the North side of Flint which was arguably the toughest side of town. Flint in itself is a tough town to live in economically and socially. It is always ranked highest or close to the highest in unemployment and crime rate per ca pita of all the cities in the United states of America and that was the same case back when I grew up there as well. It seemed like every day in the news there was a murder.

There was always someone we all knew locally being arrested and sent to jail. Luckily for me, I was somewhat afforded what I like to call a humbled beginning and lifestyle. My mom tried to give me everything I needed and everything I wanted especially since I was her youngest. In fact it seemed like everybody treated me a little bit more special because I was the youngest. Mama always went out of her way to protect me. She has always been my rock. My father on the other hand was an alcoholic who was very abusive and in particular towards my mama. Eventually mama got fed up with his abuse. She got herself a job at a factory and began saving up money.

Even though it was tough at times, she kept grinding and grinding because that's just how my mom is. As I tell you this story even now, I realize and appreciate mama even more than ever because I could not have gotten through what I went through had I not had her not only as a great mother but also as a great role model. She defined strength and perseverance. She wanted to move on and start a new life and she was going to have it no matter what. She was determined. She instilled those qualities in me to which I carry with me this very day. After saving up enough money, she packed hers and our things, all 6 of us kids and finally moved out on her own. She was a strong, independent woman who was relentless in her efforts to make a better life for us.

Mama was so resilient that she even started buying up real estate to earn extra income to help her children. She would either sell the properties or rent them out. Either way, it was her way of bringing in extra money. That's why I say I come from a humbled beginning especially considering how hard things were and still are in Flint, Michigan. By now, the whole world should know about the recent Flint Water Crisis unless you have been living under a rock or in a cave. That situation is only a small glimpse into what Flint was like growing up for me and my family but mama was always determined to give us the best she could offer within the limitations of a bad economy and a crime stricken city.

Even when it came to feeding us, she always made sure we had enough to eat especially considering how much food I could put away. Now to be honest, I have always been a big person. As a kid I was big for my age. Between the ages of 7-9 years old I had already reached 200 pounds in weight. By the age of 11, I was standing 5'10 wearing a size 12 shoe and weighing 217 pounds. I grew up with a strong and heavy dose of self esteem issues concerning my appearance. One time mama was so concerned about my self esteem that she put me on a diet consisting of chicken, water and vegetables for the whole summer. She pushed me and pushed me to the limits. She had me doing exercise regimens and everything and eventually I lost about 60 pounds that summer. That following school year I reached an idea weight to play on the football team. This fueled a confidence inside me that was always there waiting to explode. I never lacked confidence in myself. I always believed I could do any and everything I put my mind to. I just had self esteem issues about my weight but I always had an outgoing personality.

This outgoing persona kept me in a mindset of being sorta like a standout among the crowds. You see, I used to entertain my friends and my dad's friends. My dad and his friends used to give me 25 cents for performing. I was not a shy kid at all. Because of my outgoing personality, I found myself always being the go to guy so to speak. I was more like the leader of the pack kind of kid. I kinda used my size and popularity to get some of the things I wanted. So I guess you can say it was more or less like a humble bullying. I was not a bully at all but my size was intimidating and I was always humble with it though.

Now as for my brothers and sisters, we all got along pretty good. I was more close to my older sister. Being the youngest, they all kind of looked out for me and protected me even though I was so big but my biggest sister was more of a role model for me. I always looked up to her. She had this type of personality when we were growing up where she seemed authoritative but not always in a bossy way but with a commanding type of presence. When she said "do something" you just knew from the way her voice sounded that you better do it. When mama was away, she was basically our mama in her absence.

My sister is a very beautiful woman. Her name is Sherry. She used to be a model. She was very talented and would make her own clothes and always kept herself looking good. Men were always attracted to her. As my sister grew older however, she started to be attracted to the streets more-so. There were about 11 female cousins in our family who played a major role in influencing my sister. They all hung together most of the time growing up. Some of these cousins were bad influences which led my sister to the streets. They usually hung around drug dealers and thugs and always wanted her to hang out with them. Because of my large size for my age, soon my sister began to have me hang out with her in the streets mainly to watch her back while she turned tricks with Johns. I am able to tell you about her past in full disclosure with her blessing because she wanted to help you understand how her life and decisions impacted mine.

Now, early on I didn't fully understand that she was turning tricks. I never personally met any of the men she was with and to be honest, I didn't really care to meet any of them or to know what was going on. All I knew was that I was told to make sure nobody comes to interrupt her while she was doing what she was doing. She would pay me about 20-30 dollars and told me to keep quiet and continue to watch her back. This was exciting to me because I wasn't really doing anything but keeping watch for her so it felt to me like I was making easy money so it was very beneficial for me at that time.

Now, during all this time, I had no idea that my sister was doing heroine. What I did notice is that her demeanor started changing. As a young adolescent starting puberty, I didn't really know enough about life to recognize that drugs was causing this change in my sister. I mean, even though she was always a giving type of person, I could tell she started changing the way she treated me and my siblings, more-so them than me though. Nonetheless, she was still someone I looked up to. She taught me how to be tough. She basically showed me the ropes of the streets by making me hang with her.

After a while, she eventually started spending more time with what can be called a consistent John. He was a rich white man whose family came from a prominent background. His father was a rich architect from Flushing, Michigan who designed many of the newer houses in the Flushing and surrounding areas. She started seeing him more regularly even though he was actually married. I had no idea that by her turning him into a consistent John, someday her decisions concerning this white man whom I didn't even know would change my life forever. It all happened on one single night and from that night my whole life would never be the same again.

Chapter 2
The Day That Changed My Life Forever

We all have had at least one day or event in our lives that had a great impact on us which changed our lives for better or worse. Many of us have experienced something that caused our lives to never ever be the same again. I am definitely among those people. There is one particular day in my life which will be etched in my memory forever. It changed my life completely and because of that one fateful day, I will never know what it is to live a normal life ever again. It affected who I have become, how I think, respond to situations, how I sleep and basically every aspect of my existence. I never ever in my wildest dreams imagined that I would wake up one day and live what would seems to be an everlasting nightmare. To this very day, I still have trouble living what you would call a normal life. Nothing for me can be considered as normal when everything about my life is seen through the eyes of a nightmare that can never end. All of this is directly due to my own decision to do something that would bring about this blackened abyss in solitude I have been dwelling in ever since that fateful day.

It basically started out as a normal day. I woke up with my girlfriend Tracy laying next to me. We did our normal daily routine. Nothing seemed unusual. Later on that evening, me and my homeboy LJ were at the crib chilling with our women. I was in my room with Tracy and he was in his room with his girlfriend. Me and Tracy were watching TV. Both of us eventually fell asleep and then all of a sudden there was a knock at the door. We both were awakened by the knock. I leaned halfway up from my laying position and said, damn, who is that knocking on the door this late? Tracy slowly rolled over and looked at the clock and said, "It's 1:32 in the morning. You know it's your damn crazy ass sister. Baby, don't answer it. Just pretend like we are sleep and maybe her ass will just go the fuck away". As soon as she said that, Sherry, who Tracy and I both believed was at the door knocked again. Then after a brief pause, she knocked on our bedroom window and said with a commanding voice, "Open the door, I know y'all asses are in there. Open the fuckin door". Then Tracy shrugged her shoulders at me as if to say "now what". She looked at me and I knew what was going through her mind. Her shoulder shrug said what her mouth wouldn't say which was ignore Sherry and lay down and go back to sleep.

Knowing exactly how Tracy is, I could tell that she was getting pissed off. Then right at that moment she said to me "See, I told you it was her". She then turned away from me with an intense movement of obvious anger because she knew I was going to respond to my sister. That's when I said, baby, the car is out there. She knows somebody is home. I know my sister. She's going to keep knocking until somebody let her in. Tracy then turned back toward me and said, "Baby, I'm telling you, don't let her ass in. She don't bring nothing but trouble. You act like she got some kind of control over you or something". Then she turned toward the opposite side away from me again and kinda threw the covers over her head in a sorta angry way and said, "Damn". You see, what my girlfriend didn't understand is that my sister has this way about her that is kinda bossy.

Everybody in our family knows when she gets in her boss mode, we don't ask questions. We just do what she say because we know she means it. Its not that we were scared of her or nothing. Let me just put it to you this way. She sounds real intimidating to the point that even school teachers didn't want to get on her bad side. She just had this real manly type of toughness about her even though she was actually a very beautiful woman. Like, I said before, she used to model and could have went on to make a career out of it had she wanted to. Nonetheless, I knew Tracy didn't understand what I understood about my sister. I knew she was mad at me so I tried to calm the situation.

I turned toward her and and put my hand on her shoulder and said; baby, what if something is wrong? I can't do my sister like that. I gotta go and see what she want. She just basically said uhmmm hummm and gave me the cold shoulder. I got up and started to put on my pants and heard Sherry knocking again. Feeling that it must be an emergency for her to keep knocking, I hurried up and put my pants on and hustled to the door. As I was getting close to the door, I yelled out; who is it? Then while she was still knocking on the door she said; "Open the door". I opened it and said; whats up. She seemed really intense. She said; "Bay Bay, I need you to come with me. I got some stuff, I got some stuff, and I need you to come and help me with it because its too heavy for me. Its worth about 6 to 800$. I'm going to cut you in on some of the money if you help me, now come on. Hurry up, shit"! I said, what stuff are you talking about and then she said, "I got some TV's, guns, a coin collection and a bunch of art paintings".

I admit, I was excited while not knowing where or how she got hold of the stuff. I said; what, where is it at? Sherry then said, "it's at the house, you gonna come with me and go get it"? I stood there for a few seconds thinking. Then I glanced at Sherry and I could see in her eyes that she was getting impatient. One thing I had learned from hanging in the streets with my sister is that when she gives you that intense look, then you know she is serious. I wisely knew that any extra seconds of delayed response from me would inflame the situation so I quickly responded.

I told her to hold up because I was going to try to get LJ to come and go with us. She said; "ok bet, hurry up". Then I went down the hallway to LJ's room and knocked on the door. LJ said "whats up?" I said, Sherry got some stuff we gotta go get. We gotta go with her. He said "what stuff"? I told him it was some TV's guns, coin collections and shit like that. It seemed like all he heard was me saying coin collections. He said "did you say coin collections"? I could hear Sherry yelling down the hall saying "come on now damn, we gotta hurry the fuck up out of here". Then I said to LJ, Yea, that's

16

what she said now come on we gotta go right now man. He said ok and I could hear him promptly getting up and getting ready so I headed into my room and grabbed my shirt and coat and put them on. Me and LJ met up in the kitchen and then we went out the door and it was super dark. He went out the door first and I was right behind him and locked the door behind me.

We walked down the driveway and initially we didn't see her. I remember saying, where the fuck she go? Then we saw her sitting in the car smoking a cigarette. Once we got in the car, she told us that we can have all of the other shit. She said she just wanted the paintings. I said with a questioning response, paintings? She said "yea, I told you that. Yall gonna go with me or not?" Then I said yea, where is it at? Then she said the stuff was in Flushing. I was not happy at all. I said in a loud and disturbed demeanor, Flushing? She then proceeded to drive and said, "yeah that's where all the rich white people live. It's over this guy's house who has a lot of money". So then I was thinking in my mind, this some crazy ass shit. I asked her where was the guy at and she said he over to Janice house. That startled me for sure. Janice is one of my other sisters. I asked her was he over there right now?

She got mad at me and said, "yeah, bay bay, shit, ain't that what I just said, damn"! So now by this time I am really curious as to just what is really going on so being the inquisitive type of person I am, I had no problem with asking questions. She got quiet for a moment and LJ was sitting back there not saying anything. So then I asked, have you been there before? She said, "yeah one time but he don't let me come out there because he has his kids a lot". So I said, where the stuff at and she said it's right out by the door.

The whole time we were driving, LJ still remained quiet. Flushing is about 15 minutes from Flint. I knew we were going to an obviously mostly all white town so my mind was thinking about getting in and hurrying up and getting the fuck out of there. I broke the silence and said to her, so you got everything by the door? I could feel the anxiety and irritability in her voice as she responded by saying, "I done been out there already, I got everything. It's right outside the door, I'm telling you I got everything". That's when we pulled up into the driveway of a colonial style mansion. I was a beautiful house. I remember looking around at all of the other houses too and was in awe of how rich everyone must have been.

Sherry got out of the car and hurried to the back door. She went inside and literally after about 10 seconds she came out the back door with a big painting and said to us with an emphatic sound in her voice, "this is mine". By this time we had already exited the car and were walking toward her. LJ walked right past her and went straight into the house with me following right behind him. As we got inside, true enough just as she had said, everything was right by the door. We saw 2 televisions and 5 guns. There was a 357, 38, 32, a Tommy gun, and a 12 gage shotgun. There were two more paintings. On the kitchen counter we saw that there was what appeared to be a treasure box. I asked Sherry what was in the box? She told me that it was some coins. Sherry opened up the box and me and LJ looked at the coins as she grabbed two more paintings and headed to the car. Me and LJ continued to look at the coins. Sherry came back into the door and looked pissed off at the fact that we were still looking at the coins and said "Lets, go." If y'all want the rest of this stuff y'all better get it and lets go".

I grabbed the bigger TV and carried it to the trunk of the car. LJ grabbed the coin collection and the guns and wrapped them in a blanket and put them in the car. I came in and grabbed the other TV and put it in the car. LJ then went and got in on the other side of the car into the back seat. I jumped in passenger seat in the front with Sherry and then she drove off. Once we took off Sherry told me that she has to put

18

the stuff somewhere. I sat there and thought for a moment. Then I told her that she can just take it over to my house and then come back and get her stuff after she take the man back his car. So then we headed back to my house which was on Holbrook St. Finally after what seemed like a very long drive, we made it to my house. As soon as we arrived we then unloaded the stuff and put it in the guest room.

My sister grabbed 2 paintings. I went back outside to the car to see what was left and I saw a painting and grabbed it and came back into the house and headed down to the basement. Sherry stood at the top of the steps and as soon as I started walking back up the steps she said to me, "Let me tell you something motherfucka, my painting better be here when I get back". I told her don't nobody want that shit. I guess I didn't think about the value of the painting because I was more concerned about how much we could get after we sold the other stuff. Then in that same emphatic yet forceful voice she let me know that she knows LJ got that coin collection because she knew that he kept looking at it. She said to me "don't make me have to fuck y'all up".

While all of this was going on, LJ was in the kitchen making some koolaid. Sherry just stayed near the back door waiting on us. Then she said to me, "Bay bay, I need y'all to come with me. I'm scared to take the car back by myself. He gonna know, He gonna know". That caused me to start getting very worried and concerned because I didn't want me and LJ's girlfriends to know that we stole some shit. I made a motion with my fingers to my lips to tell her to be quiet. Sherry looked at me and I pointed to my bedroom to let her know my woman was in there probably listening. She understood what I was trying to say and kept quiet. LJ was finishing up with making the koolaid so I told him that we needed to head outside. LJ grabbed his coat. Me and Sherry had already started walking toward the back porch.

While we were making our way toward the back porch Sherry said "Bay Bay, he gonna know I did it". So I said who, and she said "Freddy". I said, who the fuck is Freddy? She said, "my trick". I asked her where was he at and she said that he was over to my sister Janice house. That's when I said, Oh no, so we gotta get him the fuck out of there then. I asked her should I get my gun and she said no. As I was about to hop into his car, she said no, I don't want him to see y'all in the car. My car was sitting on the curb so I went and hopped into my car. I was just ready to hurry up and get that shit done and over with so I could get back home to my girl. LJ got in the car with me and we took off. We followed behind but not too far behind her as we headed over to my sister Janice's house. Finally we arrived at her house on Russel st. Sherry got out of Freddy's car and walked up the back steps. Me and LJ just stayed put. We sat there for a few seconds and then we got out of the car. I said to LJ, grab a joint man. I looked over toward the house and all I could see is nothing but darkness. The only light was a light from the stove in the kitchen. I wasn't sure if Janice was in there or not.

LJ decided of all times that he had to take a leak so we went around to the back porch to find somewhere that he could piss without someone in the neighborhood seeing us and getting suspicious about anything. As you can already assume, I was extremely paranoid at this time and every sound including the night owls would have been an alarming sound to me. I just knew at that time that Sherry needed to hurry up and come on so we could get the hell out of there with the quickness. I saw a tree that looked like it was the perfect spot for LJ to take a piss so I pointed it out to him and he went over to it to handle his business. It was rather cold out that night so, it didn't take him long to finish up. He went toward the house and said he was about to go see whats taking Sherry so damned long. I didn't blame him because I was cold as hell and nervous as all get up and was ready to get the hell up out of there. He went in there and was stunned at what he saw.

What he saw would change his life and mine forever.

Sherry was sitting on the floor. She was sitting up against the couch is a daze. She was is in disbelief of what she had just done. She was breathing heavily and she was crying. LJ. later said that he stood there just staring momentarily unable to move a muscle of his mouth to say anything so he said that he put his hand over his mouth as if to keep from saying anything out loud. He said that finally, he broke his silence and started yelling at Sherry. I could hear him yelling out "what the fuck did you do, bitch is you crazy" as he came running out of the house. Once he got out side he was yelling saying "the bitch is crazy man, that bitch is crazy. The bitch killed him".

I was definitely startled because I definitely wasn't expecting to hear that shit. Those words coming out of his mouth have haunted me to this day and will haunt me for the rest of my life. No one can really understand how I felt at that very moment. I became overtaken by extreme anxiety. My adrenaline began to overflow in production at that point and so I ran inside the house as if I was Carl Lewis in the Olympics to see if what he had just told me was true. He came running in right behind me. As soon as I got inside the house my eyes instantly became widened in total disbelief at what I saw. God, damn was the first thought that flowed through my mind. I couldn't process what I was actually seeing right before my very eyes. She actually killed this man. I was in total shock. I mean, I was so much in shock that I literally stopped in my tracks and didn't move an inch forward. I felt paralyzed and couldn't move a muscle.

It was dark in there but let me tell you, what I saw was shining through all of the darkness. I continued to stare in horror. As I stared in shock, my eyes went into a state of blurred disbelief also. As my eyes started to weaken from disbelief, all I could really make out at that point was a silhouette of a huge motionless body laying on his back. LJ was standing right there behind me. He looked at Sherry while she was still sitting there crying with her back up against the couch holding a hammer. She definitely seemed like she was in some kind of zombie type of daze way far worse than what I was in. It was as if she had stepped outside of herself and outside of the realm of reality and went into a deep deep trance. It was almost like she was having an out of body experience and looking in shock at her other self.

She was only a few feet away from the man's body. Then in an instant she mumbles to me while crying saying "he's dead Bay Bay, he's dead". She was sitting right directly near the man's head and upper torso. While crying even harder, she started yelling out saying "what have I done, what have I done"? At that very moment I knew I had to take charge of the situation or things could get out of hand because I felt that it was quite obvious my sister was on the brink of losing it. I didn't want the next door neighbors to hear her yelling. I managed to get the courage to break from my own state of shock and walked towards him while stepping over Sherry's legs. As I looked at the body, I saw a broken iron laying by his head. I even saw shattered pieces of the iron laying all over the place. I remember thinking to myself, damn, this is some fucked up shit.

I looked at my sister and again said to her, what the fuck you done did? This made her cry even much more harder. In my humble opinion I kinda suspected that her ass was probably high on some heroine or some other shit and realized that I was not going to get any answers from her. This shit was just too unbelievable. I mean, how in hell did I find myself in this situation and how in hell was I going to rectify it. The dude looked dead and so I knew we needed to do something and do something really quick. I looked directly at his head and I saw all of the blood all over his head. I knelt down to check to see if he had a heart beat and didn't hear anything. I turned toward Sherry and said, oh he's dead alright". Then Sherry started crying even more harder.

All I remember thinking is that we needed to leave before someone hears her ass making all that damned noise with her loud ass crying. I turned to LJ and said, man we gotta get him out of here. LJ said, "man, I'm not touching him". Although I realized that the whole situation was crazy as hell, I knew we couldn't get caught up in Janice's house under these circumstances. I said to LJ, look man, we gotta get him out of Janice's house. Janice is gonna get in trouble for this shit. Then I took another look at the body to try and figure out how to remove it from the area. I looked at LJ and I said: go get some garbage bags.

While he went to get the bags I looked at Sherry who had stopped crying at that point. I noticed her head was bobbing up and down as if she was sleeping or having some kind of anxiety attack or something. At first I thought she was losing her damned mind. In actuality she was having a nervous breakdown so I guess in a way I was kinda right. She was literally losing her damned mind. The main thing I kept concentrating on the whole time however, was getting the hell up out of there and with the quickness. Finally, LJ came back with the trash bags and handed them to me. I took them and then I started staring at the body assessing the situation. I had to figure out how I was going to try to stuff the body into the bags. I told LJ to go get some rope. He asked me where was the rope? I said to him, I don't know, go check the basement. He went to the basement to look for it.

While he went to look for the rope, I opened up one of the garbage bags and stood over the victim. I remember cautiously stepping over the blood and attempted to put his head into the garbage bag. He was more heavier than I thought and I figured out with the quickness that trying to do that shit alone was going to be more difficult than I thought. I realized I needed help. I figured I needed to go get LJ so I stepped over a pool of blood with one leg, and then suddenly I see one of his arms reaching up. He grabbed one of my pants legs. Man, let me tell you, I was so horrified. I mean, I thought this dude was dead. I damn near tripped out on that. My whole body went numb. Then what freaked me out even more is that I faintly heard him saying; "Help me, help me".

To be honest I don't know if I slipped into a twilight zone or what. I mean, the whole damn thing seemed unreal. I remember turning to Sherry and calling out her name. Sherry, Sherry. She looked up at me but didn't say anything. She was obviously still in shock about what she had just done. I yelled out for LJ telling him to come here. He came back into the area holding a clothesline in his hand and said;"what". I said, man, he ain't dead. He looked down at him and said, "oh he is dead man, look at him. He is not moving". I said man, I'm telling you he just moved. He got on the floor and listened to the man's heartbeat and said, "I don't hear nothing". At that point I figured I must have been imagining what I thought happened. I said to LJ, when I lift him up, then you put the garbage bags over him. Then I said to him, here use this to tie him up as I handed him the rope. LJ started to tie him up but I could tell that he was having a difficult time so I took the clothes line from him and I began to tie his feet and hands together. He asked me what was I doing that for and I told him that I was doing it so that it would make it easier to carry the body if his feet and hands were tied together.

I put my hands under Mr Wellington's arm pits and lifted him up slightly. Then LJ placed one of the garbage bags over his head and slid it over the body. I laid him back down onto the floor. Then LJ pulled the bag the rest of the way over the body. Now, I know a lot of you are probably judging me as you are reading this and thinking I am a horrible person. Most of you will immediately think that I should have went to the police and turned my sister in and I would not have been in

24

any part of a conspiracy from the beginning. I want you to think about it from my perspective as I was in a critical situation filled with panic, anxiety, emotion, concern, fear and so much more.

Keep in mind that my sister was from the streets and taught me the street code which is a language of understanding that people of the streets know and it is an unwritten code. I knew this code and I knew that I had to live by that code or I was going to die by that code. In the streets, you simply have each other back. You didn't see what you really saw and you didn't hear what you really heard. I had to honor that code and I had to help my sister get rid of the body not only to honor the code but more importantly, I had to protect my sister and my own life too. Remember, you either live by the code or you die by the code.

After we finished putting him in the bag, I noticed some sheets laying on the floor in the hallway going toward the bedroom. I went and got them and went over to Sherry and told her that we gotta clean this stuff up. We gotta clean this blood up. She still had that hammer clinched in her hands. Then all of a sudden, within an instant she hopped up and became her old self again and started giving orders to me and LJ. She told me to go and get some bleach. Then she went and got a mop bucket and filled it with hot water and soap and set it in the living room near the body. She went into the bathroom and grabbed some towels and came back to the living room and tossed the towels to me. I started wiping the blood and realized that it was not coming up and so I told her that we needed some brushes.

She went into the kitchen and came back quickly with some scouring pads. She threw them to me and I started scrubbing the blood from the carpet. LJ came back in and started helping me clean up. I looked around and noticed that Sherry was no longer in the area where I could see or hear her so I turned to LJ and said, we gotta go, we gotta get him out of here. Go open up the trunk. He went toward the kitchen and walked out of the back door. He opened the trunk and came back into the living room. He told me that he had the trunk open so I told him to help me grab him. I reached down and grabbed Mr. Wellington by his torso. He was a very heavy man so it was taking me a minute to adjust my grip on him. LJ saw me struggling and grabbed his legs. We started dragging him from the living room toward the kitchen area which led to the back door. We paused for a second. LJ said that maybe we needed to pull the car closer to the door because we wouldn't want the neighbors to see us loading a dead body into the car. I thought that was a great idea, so we gently set the body down and he went and moved the car closer. While he went to move the car, I looked around the proximity and still didn't see my sister. I remember wondering, where in the hell is she?

Finally, LJ came back after having moved the car and told me that he had the car parked right at the steps to the back door. I said ok cool, let's get him in here so we can bust up out of here. We proceeded to load him in the trunk of the car. After we got him securely into the back trunk, LJ slammed it shut and we went back into the house toward the living room. At that point, Sherry had finally made her way back to the living room and was on the floor on her knees scrubbing up the blood. She looked at me and LJ with a firm, stern yet angry voice telling us that we better not say anything to nobody. She warned us that if we opened our mouths then we all would go down. Then she went to the bathroom to dump the bucket of bloody water into the toilet. Me and LJ went to the kitchen.

Sherry came out of the bathroom and came into the kitchen and looked at me and LJ and said with that same stern forceful voice, "I mean it God Dammit, y'all better not say anything". Me and LJ just stood there in silence. It was almost as if Sherry was our mama telling us what to do and what not to do. The crazy thing about it is that I felt scared enough to

26

obey her as if she was my mom. She always had that strong of a personality which I looked up to. She told me that I had to get rid of the car so I told her that I would take it up to Pierson school. She told me not to take it to the school. She said to take it over on Sherman street and drop it off in front of the dope house. LJ asked her why did she want to drop it off at the dope house and I told him that maybe by putting the car there, it will look like someone at the dope house killed him.

LJ was really eager to get the hell up out of there so he went outside and started up Mr. Wellington's car. I heard the engine running and that was my cue to get up out of there too. As I was going to the car, Sherry told me that she would meet us at my house. I asked her how long was she going to be and she said that she would be maybe about 10 minutes or so. I jumped in my car and started it up and began pulling out of the driveway. LJ followed behind me in Mr. Wellington car. After driving a little ways and making a few turns, I looked in rear view mirror to make sure LJ was still following me. Finally, we turned onto Sherman street. I parked about 4 houses before the dope house. I looked around to see if traffic was going in and out of the dope house. I was trying to make sure that no one saw me pulling up. I also looked around the perimeter to make sure that no one was outside standing around to witness anything. I got out of my car and walked over to the car LJ was driving.

LJ rolled down the window to see what I wanted. I pointed towards the dope house. LJ was looking kinda baffled so I told him to take the car and park it over there at the yellow house. He rolled up the window up and I walked off while looking over my shoulder, I see LJ driving by. I watched his and my back as he parked the car in front of the yellow house as I had told him. LJ got out of the car and left the keys in the ignition and ran across the street to my car and jumped in. We then drove off heading to my house.

27

At that point, I remember looking backwards over my shoulder at the car and started reflecting. I started thinking to myself, wow, there's a body in that car. I felt a huge sense of guilt and became highly stressed at that moment. I continued to drive though but the whole while I still kept looking at the rear view mirror periodically. As we got near Ruth street I noticed someone walking and realized that it was my sister walking down the street towards us. I slowed down and pulled up to her. I rolled down my window and told her to get in the car so we could take her home. She said no and said she had somewhere else to go first. I didn't really understand what she had to do that was so important but to be honest, I really was more concerned about getting back to the safety and comfort of my house.

I just wanted to hurry up and get off the road before anybody discovered that body and could possibly remember seeing me driving in the area. Finally after a drive which seemed to take forever, we pulled up to my house. We didn't want to awaken our women so we went in through the back door. I told LJ to go and check and see if his girl was still asleep and I did the same. LJ came out of his room and went into kitchen and sat at kitchen table. I went into my room and saw that my girl was still sleeping. I closed the bedroom door quietly and went to the kitchen and sat at the table with LJ. I lit up the unfinished joint I had in my pocket. I needed to mellow out because I was extremely tense. I couldn't believe what had just happened. That night changed my life forever.

Chapter 3
Getting Rid Of The Evidence

Me and LJ were both shell shocked over what we had just been through. We both were sitting in silence and passing the joint back and forth that we had just lit up. Just as we were finishing the joint we heard a soft knock at the back door. LJ got up and opened the door. It was Sherry. She came in and didn't say nothing to either one of us and just boldly walked directly down the basement. I got up and walked to the steps and stood at the top of the stairs waiting for Sherry to come up but to no avail. That's when I kinda got irritated and I looked at LJ and told him, Oh, she's not staying here. He asked why not? I said because she is high. I went and sat back at the table and we both continued to just sit there in complete silence.

After a few minutes had passed, Sherry finally came up from the basement. She told us that she was going to take one of the paintings with her and that she was going to leave the others there at my house. I looked her directly into her eyes and I could tell that she seemed even higher than she was before she went down the basement. I knew right then that she went downstairs to shoot another fix of heroine. She took the painting and headed to the back door. She turned towards LJ and me and gave us that bossy stern look again and said, "Remember what I told you motherfuckas. You better not say nothing". Then she walked out the door with the painting.

I went to the living room and looked out the front window to see if Sherry had a ride waiting on her. Within in seconds, she came from the side of the house. I kept watching her. As soon as she reached the intersection I saw her getting into a white 1967 four door Ford Thunderbird with suicide doors. I went back into the kitchen. I said to LJ, "She gone. She took that painting with her. She got in a white Thunderbird, She gone." LJ pointed toward the basement and then asked me what are we going to do with the rest of her stuff. I told him that we would have to talk about it tomorrow. I was too stressed to worry about it at that moment. Then he said he was about to go back into the room with his girlfriend.

As he walked off, I remember talking a good look at him and I noticed how stressed he also looked. Even his body language looked stressed out. I subtly called out to him before he went into the room because I didn't want to wake the women up. I said; LJ, we good man, remember, we didn't kill nobody. He didn't say anything. He just walked on into his room. I was so worried that his facial expression and his body language would make his girl get suspicious. I turned and walked into my room and Tracy was up. I immediately began to get really really nervous because I wasn't sure if she heard anything or not. She walked out of the bathroom and asked me what's going on? At that moment I began to take off my shirt. As I pulled off my shirt from over my head, I calmly said, nothing, Sherry just up to her old tricks. She climbed into the bed and rolled over onto her side opposite of how she usually laid which was facing toward me. I knew then that she knew something wasn't right.

I hopped into the bed and I remember just staring off into the ceiling. I kept wondering what did she hear if anything at all. I just laid there in silence going through so many emotions. My mind was distressed by what had just happened. Then I started pondering hard on what we were going to do with that stuff. All I knew was that we had to get rid of it and with the quickness. My mind was racing at 90 miles per hour trying to think of all of the possible people I can sell that stuff to. What was probably only a few minutes seemed like hours until it came to me suddenly. I said to myself, maybe I can get my brother Kenny to help me get rid of this shit. Then I whispered ever so confidently saying yea, I can get Kenny. Then I closed my eyes and fell asleep.

That next morning, I got up early and called my brother Kenny and let him know I was coming over. I told LJ to come with me. We made it to his house at around 8:00. We knocked on the door and he told us to come on in. Other people were in the house so we pulled him off to the side and told him about all the stuff we had. I said; "dig this big bro, we've got some stuff we need to get rid of. He said stuff like what? I told him that we had 2 TV's 5 guns and some coins. He said he needed to look at the stuff so I told him that he would have to come to my crib to look at everything because I wasn't about to be carting that stuff around knowing it was stolen. He told me he would meet me at my house in 20 minutes. Then he told me that Sherry came to his house acting extremely nervous. He said that the first thing she blurted out of her mouth was we just killed somebody. Then Kenny said he asked her what did she mean? He said that she said that her, me and LJ had to kill somebody last night. And then he said that she said that she needed to see him later on because she had some paintings that she needed to get rid of. I said to him, yeah whatever. I didn't do nothing with her. I told him I would see him in a few minutes.

Me and LJ left his house and went home and turned on ESPN in the living room. LJ asked me did I want him to go and bring the stuff up from the basement. I told him yes and that I would be downstairs in a minute to help him. I continued to watch ESPN while he brought the stuff upstairs. By the time he had brought up the last bit of stuff, there was a knock at the door. I got up to open the door because I already knew who it was and I was right. It was in fact Kenny just as I thought. I said come on in big bro. He came in and started looking at the stuff. He said, yeah, I can get rid of this shit. He picked up two of the guns and looked at them and then paused for a moment.

Then he told me that he needed to use my phone. I asked him who was he going to be calling. He told me that he had a few people he could call. He proceeded to get my phone and called my uncle Darryl. Me and LJ stood there listening to him while he was talking to him. He told Darryl that he would have to come to the house to pick the stuff up. Darryl agreed and so they ended the call. We all continued to sit in the living

32

room watching ESPN for about a half an hour to nearly an hour. We were watching the NBA All-star preview. Finally, Darryl knocked on the door.

Still sitting on the couch watching TV, I yelled out to him to come on in. Kenny got up and went outside the door before Darryl could come inside the house. They stood out there for about 5 minutes and then they both came back in. As soon as he came in I said hi uncle Darryl to him to which he replied, "how you doing nephew, what you got for me"? I pointed to the stuff and he went over and started looking at everything. He paid a particular interest in the guns. Then Kenny told him that he could get everything for $800. Darryl looked at everything again, while still fixated on the guns and then turned toward Kenny and said that he had $700 on him and that he would bring the rest back. Kenny said ok cool and so uncle Darryl reached into his pocket and pulled out the wad of money and gave it to Kenny. We all started grabbing stuff and loaded it into the cab of Darryl's pickup truck. Once we got everything loaded, uncle Darryl left. Me, Kenny and LJ went back into the house. Kenny handed me the money. I counted it and then handed him $200 of it and said thanks. He said no problem.

I asked him what was he about to do and asked what did he have going on later on? He told me that he was going to be meeting up with Sherry later to help her get rid of the paintings. The whole time afterward I was finding myself becoming more worried and stressed out. Sherry had emphatically told me and LJ not to say anything to nobody, yet, she was going around being a blabber mouth about the whole thing. I could feel that too much attention was being drawn to us. As a way of getting away from it all, me and LJ would go to Chicago periodically. We were spending more time in Chicago than Flint. I guess in a way, I kinda knew that eventually I was going to come face to face with what had happened whether dealing with it internally or through the justice system but at that time I didn't want to deal with it. Hanging out in Chicago was my sanctuary away from my true reality. I created my own new reality and basically lived a lie.

Chapter 4
Getting Captured

The whole time while I was in Chicago, I had no idea that my sister Sherry had inadvertently said and did things that would bring me down and eventually send me to prison for nearly 27 years of my life. She couldn't seem to keep her mouth shut about what had happened that fateful night. One day, she was walking down the street and one of her friends came up to her and told her that she had seen her on the show Crime Stoppers which came on TV locally in Flint. She had been on Crime Stoppers because she was wanted by the police for escaping prison while serving time for attempted murder and arson. You see, she had previously had an altercation with one of her pimps. He shot her in her hand. She didn't report it to the police. She didn't even go to the hospital to get medical help for her gunshot wound to her hand. Instead of going to the hospital she took the bullet out herself. She had still been inflamed with anger about the fact that he shot her so she went to his house and set it aflame with him in it. He managed to get out though.

I guessed that obviously, her pimp must have gone to the police and she ended up doing prison time for arson and attempted murder. She had been later sent to a facility called New Paths which was a halfway house for inmates who were soon to be released. This type of facility allowed inmates to leave the facility on weekends and be with their families. One day Sherry left for a weekend visit and never returned back and that is the reason why there was a warrant issued for her arrest. After finding out from her friend that she had been featured on Crime Stoppers, she went and turned herself in to the authorities. She plea bargained and was doing time in prison. Some of my female cousins went up to the prison one day to visit her and she ended up telling them about the murder. I didn't find out about this until I had been arrested. She had told them not to tell anyone about the murder according to what I was told after the fact.

Now, keep in mind that this whole time after my sister

had killed Mr. Wellington, both me and LJ were under the impression that we all would keep our mouths shut about that night. Me and LJ most certainly weren't talking about it to anyone and yet my sister was just running her mouth as if she was a writer for a gossip column. There was a $1000 reward for any information leading to the arrest of anyone involved with the death of Mr. Wellington. One of those cousins who visited my sister called the Crime Stoppers hotline and turned us in and collected that money. Can you believe that? My own cousin. Now, I was still in Chicago at that time and didn't know she had turned us in until after the fact but I still felt betrayed nonetheless.

Me and LJ made our way back to Flint but we remained worried because I knew that with Sherry still running her mouth, it would eventually lead to our arrest. Because of that fact, I stayed on edge for a few weeks worried about the inevitable day when I would have to come face to face with the justice system. I feared that when that inevitable day happened, I would then have to try to prove my innocence to a system whose justice was always elusive when it comes to people of color. Every time I heard a siren, my body would tense up. Each and every day that inevitable day of capture seemed to inch closer and closer. It would seem as if with each passing day, the chances of the police investigation trail leading toward us would become colder and colder but instead, each passing day caused me to be more stressed. After a few short weeks of my being on pins and needles stressing myself out abut everything, that inevitable moment finally came.

I was at my house in bed laying next to Tracy. It was around 2:00 in the morning. I heard a knock at the door but initially just ignored it. Then there was a second knock which was even louder and more forceful sounding. I got up and walked down the hallway. I called out to LJ and asked him did he hear anything and he said no. I kept walking toward the living room which led to the front door. Then suddenly I heard a sound from behind me. It sounded like a loud motor had just fired up. I rushed to the front door and just as I got about 5 feet from the door, the damned door came crashing inward toward me. The first thing I remember thinking is "what the fuck".

Then the reality of everything became so clear. There were at least 21 police officers in full riot gear rushing through my front and back doors. All I heard was get on the floor, get on the floor now. Tracy came running out of the room screaming as they again repeated the same command to me and then directly to her shouting even louder than before. "Get on the floor, get on the floor". She kept screaming "what did I do, what did I do". With their guns pointed directly at her face, they shouted again to her, "get down on the floor now". As I began to throw my hands up in the surrender position, I glanced over at her and saw the terror in her eyes as I listened to the frantic sounds and trauma coming from her voice.

By this time, other officers had already made their way into the house from the back door. As I was dropping to my knees with my hands up in the air, I could hear LJ's girlfriend screaming out saying on Tracy's behalf "she's not in this, she don't know nothing". I laid on the floor faced downward. That's when at least 7 or 8 shotguns were immediately pointed at my head. I glanced over at Tracy and saw her screaming frantically with tears streaming from her eyes. It was kinda hard to worry about my own fate at that very moment because all I could think about was her and how this was affecting her. I mean, she was an innocent victim and because of my decisions, she had all of those Police in her house with their guns drawn and they had her laying on the floor as if she was some kind of criminal. It was kinda like having an out of body experience. I mean, don't get me wrong. I understood the magnitude of what was happening to myself but it was as if I was hovering above everything and looking at myself and

Tracy and seeing the whole scene play out.

They took out a picture and leaned me a little bit upward from the floor and said, yeah, it's him. Suddenly, Tracy started screaming "what did you do, what did you do?" My face took on a grave yet shame filled look after hearing her ask me that. I knew I couldn't answer her right then and there and yet, she didn't deserve to be in the dark about what was going on. They handcuffed me and stood me up. By the time I had stood up, I saw LJ being led toward the front door in handcuffs. As they were pushing me out the door, I glanced back and saw a female cop helping Tracy up off the floor. The last thing I saw before being led out was her face filled with tears as she continued to sob in disbelief at what was happening. I watched them as they led LJ to a separate police car from the one I was in. It was in the middle of winter and I didn't have on a shirt or any shoes. All I had on was some blue jeans. I asked the officer, can I at least get a coat? I looked at the lieutenant and I could tell that my question pissed him off because his green eyes started to turn bloodshot red. Then the lieutenant said, "Why should you have a coat, Mr Wellington didn't have a coat. He laid there frozen to death".

Right then and there I knew it was going to be an uphill battle fighting these charges and fighting the system. They had me convicted without a trial, without even hearing my side of the story. I mean, what ever happened to the notion of being innocent until proven guilty? They treated me like I had already seen a jury, been convicted and escaped from prison and was finally caught. I think it was at that very moment when I started suspecting that somehow, Justice was going to become my enemy. I was seeing a different kind of justice that most who are accused of a crime are forced to see that is so different from what we are always taught is justice. Nonetheless, there was a feeling of relief that had come over me as the police car I was in began to drive off. I knew I didn't have to run anymore. That part of the stress I was under was finally over. Because I was innocent and because I thought that my sister would take care of everything, I just kinda wanted to hurry up and get this phase of the process over with so I could move on with my life. After they forced us into the respective cars, they drove off with seemingly triumphant and boastful swagger.

As we moved closer to downtown Flint, Michigan, I could hear the lieutenant get on the police radio talking to the car that was transporting LJ telling them to take Saginaw street and that he would take MLK which was Martin Luther King St. This seemed like it was the longest ride I had ever taken in my entire life up to that point. I just wanted all this mess to hurry up and be over with. Have you ever been so overwhelmed with stress to the extent that you couldn't even show any emotions? I think we all have experienced something similar to that feeling whether it was fear, grief, anger, and perhaps even uncertainty about your circumstances. Well, that is pretty much what I was going through as the police car pulled up in the parking lot that led to the city jail. As we pulled into the back of the Police Department, I noticed tons of News reporters and cameras. And get this, it seemed as if the entire Police department was standing outside waiting on our arrival. They were all standing there and cheering as we pulled up. That sorta fueled my suspicions into a firm belief at that point that Justice had in fact become my enemy. They had already achieved what in their hearts and minds was their kind of justice. They believed I killed that man and was cheering my capture without even knowing if I was even ever at the scene of the crime.

My confidence in my sister at that time however, wouldn't allow me to fall too deep into despair because she was my ace in the hole to get me out of this mess I found myself in. I had to hurry up and get myself ready for that moment when I would eventually have to get out of the car and reveal myself to a mob of reporters but instead, I instantly became emotionless. I couldn't grieve even though I was devastated. I couldn't show how scared I was because I didn't want to be viewed as an easy target for bullying. I couldn't cry because I didn't want to show weakness. I couldn't show bravery because I didn't want to appear cocky. My heart was numb and my mind was blank. In those few short moments before being pulled from the police car, I reflected back on my whole life and saw all of my hopes and dreams possibly being washed away. It was as if I had zoned out of reality and was existing in a world I couldn't believe was real but yet it felt so real. It was kinda like that out of body experience I had earlier when I watched Tracy lay on the floor in terror so to speak.

I looked around and all I saw was this fortress that I was about to be led into against my will. Here I was about to turn 19 years old and hadn't even really experienced life but yet I found myself facing the possibility of life in prison and what made it worse was that it was all because of my own choices. I chose to ride with my sister to steal something that night and then I was the one who chose to look out for my sister and concealed a murder. You see, in the streets everyone knows the unwritten code of honor that you live by. You don't tell on each other. That's just the way the street game is played. Then that moment finally arrived.

They walked around to my door and my heart began racing because at that moment I was realizing that this is real and I am no longer a free man able to do what I want to do and go where I want to go. The lieutenant came over to the passenger door where I was sitting and as he opened the door, a reporter placed a microphone into the lieutenant's face after having said, "you've finally made an arrest". The lieutenant replied by saying, "it was just a matter of time". The reporter then asked if they could get a statement. The lieutenant replied by saying, "There will be other arrests. We will be making a statement and taking questions this afternoon".

They pulled me out of the police car and while at the same time pulling LJ out of the other car. There I was hopping out of a police car with my hands cuffed behind my back and why? I'll tell you why. It was because I was not only just trying to uphold an unwritten street code, I was protecting my sister. In my mind I had done the right thing by helping her get rid of the body because I didn't want her to go to jail. To be honest, if I had the chance to do it all over again, I would still do the same thing. That's just the nature of my character. I would rather go down than to let my sister go down because I looked up to her. The sad part about it though, is the fact that I never thought in my wildest dreams that she would break the street code and throw me under the bus as we say in the streets. As they escorted me into the station, I tried to muster up every ounce of strength I had left in me needed to hold myself together and keep my emotions in check. I needed them to see that I was just an ordinary good guy who didn't deserve to be in this predicament.

We entered the Police station through the same door but they immediately separated me and LJ sending us to separate rooms. This was a tactic to keep us from concocting a story. Once they got me into a room, it took a few minutes for them to come back in. Finally, lieutenant Jay Espy came in and sat down directly in front of me and just stared directly into my eyes with a glaring stern look on his face. He was sizing me up and so I stared right back at him as if to say to him I'm also **was** sizing you up too. He placed a tape recorder on the table while still maintaining his glaring stare. Then with a cocky, arrogant and confident tone of voice he said, "would you like to make a confession seeing how your sister has made a confession and Mr. Wilson is also confessing as we speak"?

I sat there and paused for a few seconds and then told him that I really didn't know what to say. He then pressed play on the tape and I sat there and listened to it. When I heard my sisters testimony, my body stiffened up as if I was a deer standing in the midst of an oncoming car's headlights. I was in total shock at what I was hearing. It was Sherry and she was telling the most bold faced lie that I had ever heard from anyone's mouth ever in my entire life. Oh my God, I couldn't believe the crap that was spewing from my sister's mouth. Listen to what she had the nerve to say.

She said and I quote: "You don't know my brother. He's big and he's crazy. He's going to kill me. Maurice is the one that hit Mr. Wellington repeatedly with an iron at first. Then he hit him with the hammer". The whole time I was sitting there, I was in total disbelief. I was so angry at her that I really can't put into words what was going through my mind at that time. I mean, can you believe this shit? She was painting me out to be some kind of viscous brute and ring leader and the whole time, she was describing exactly the type of person she was and how she had been toward people all of her life. She was basically telling the real story but only using my name in place of hers. I mean, this is supposed to be my flesh and blood sister.

Disbelief then turned into numbness all over again. I really didn't know what to think or say but then quickly realized that I was definitely in a no win situation. I didn't even think about asking for a lawyer or nothing. I just froze in a state of confusion trying to understand why Sherry and LJ had even talked to the police in the first place and wondered what were they going to do to me now. The lieutenant pressed stop on the tape and looked me straight in the eyes and asked me again, "would you like to tell your side of the story now?" I looked at him and asked him just what did he want me to say? He put in a blank tape and pressed record and that's when I decided that I had to defend my right to be free. I gave my confession. Lieutenant Peek looked at me and said, "You are doing the right thing son. You are doing the right thing."

I messed up and talked to him and years later I realized the magnitude of that mistake. I told my side of the story not knowing what leverage he had. All I knew is that I needed to tell the truth because my sister certainly wasn't telling the truth. LJ said I killed that man too and so that left me in a serious tight spot. Next thing I knew, the interview was over and what seemed like only 20 minutes actually took 3 hours. Then he said with that same cocky and arrogant voice, "We have enough testimony from Mr Wilson and your sister Sherry to send you to prison for the rest of your life." I remember just sitting there contemplating while my heart was racing rapidly.

Immediately after the interview was over, the officers stood me up. In their minds, my statement was all they needed to hear and they used it to place me into permanent custody. In that moment I knew they were certain that they were going to charge me with something which I thought at minimum was going to be failure to report a crime. Jay Espy told them to handcuff me. The officer then said the most dreadful words that still haunt me to this day. He said, "Mr Maurice Moore, You are under arrest." Those are words that I will never forget as long as I exist on earth. Then he put those tight metal handcuffs on me and took me into custody. My head bowed down in disbelief at what was happening to me at that moment.

Then lieutenant Peek put his hand on my shoulder and said, "its ok son, it's ok." Then they escorted me out of that room to take me to the county jail. As we were walking out of the door and down the hallway, LJ was being escorted out of the room he had been in. He didn't even make eye contact with me at all. I did see his face however and he had a very sad depressed and stressed look on his face. They put us both in the same car and took us a few blocks down the street transporting us from the city jail to the county jail. While en route to the county jail, the officer told me that I would never see the light of day again. 1st degree murder carries a mandatory life sentence. Lieutenant Jay Espy wanted to rub all of this in my face so when it came time for my arraignment, he made sure he was the one who took me instead of letting a deputy do it which is the common practice. For his showboating, he was promoted to Captain and only remained at that position for 9 months and was then appointed Chief of police by the mayor and all because of him being the one who brought me, my sister and LJ into custody.

This case was highly publicized for some reason which years later I found out why. It was because Mr Wellington belonged to a prominent family. Once we arrived at the arraignment, Jay Espy reiterated his statement to me saying, you'll never see the streets again. I kept thinking and believing that I was going to prove him wrong. While sitting there waiting, so many thoughts kept ringing in my mind. Why am I here? What are they going to do to me? Am I going to prison? Is mama ok? I don't want mama to worry herself to death. How did I get into this situation? How do I get myself out of this situation? Why couldn't I have just listened to Tracy and ignored my sister when I knew I should have just stayed my ass in the bed that night. Why me, damn, why me?

Then suddenly I heard that voice call out my name," Maurice Moore" and my whole body became numb all over again but at the same time very tense. It was time to walk over to the desk to get processed into the system. I had to give myself a little pep talk. Come on Maurice, it's going to be ok man. You can do this! Let's just hurry up and do this and get this shit over with. Everything is going to be ok, just calm down, just calm down, I kept saying to myself. I sat down nervous as can be but confidently believing that soon I would be able to go home because I knew I didn't kill nobody.

While they were booking me into the system and finger printing me, I kept waiting for a miracle to happen. I was hoping an officer would come in and and stop the process and say that they got the wrong man. That miracle never happened and finally it was time for them to take me to my holding cell.

45

LJ was put in a cell three spaces from me. I remember walking into that bull pin which is another name for the holding cell. The county jail bull pin had always had a reputation as being a source of hell for young men such as myself at that stage of my life. So many young men in there were worried about their fate. So many men in there were angry and so many men in there were ready to try and gain some kind of power over anyone who they perceived to be weak. Everyone had to have the persona of toughness and those who were experienced in real crime knew who was fake and who was real.

That night as they put me in the bull pin, I was certainly among all of those kinds I just described. As I stated earlier, they had separated LJ and me. I was put in a cell which had 13 people and this cell was designed to hold only 5 people so you can imagine how crowded and uncomfortable I was right from the beginning. I felt crowded and I had no space to even try to become comfortable in a situation which I really wasn't trying to get comfortable with in the first place but hey, lets face it. I had to make the best of the worst situation I could ever imagined I would ever be facing. Most of the men in the county jail were in there on murder charges. You have to remember the history of Flint, Michigan at that time to understand why there were so many men in the county Jail facing murder charges.

Back in 1986, Flint had one of the highest murder rates in the entire nation. Many factors contributed to the high crime and murder rates but the number 1 and 2 reasons for it was Reaganomics and drugs. Reaganomics was the term society gave to the failed economic policies of President Reagan's administration. During that period of time, the drug known as Crack had become an epidemic which was overtaking the Flint community. It was believed by so many that Vice President George Bush was partly responsible for the drug epidemic but that's a whole other story. So there I was sitting in the bull pin with an empty feeling in my stomach but at the same time, feeling heavily weighted down both mentally and physically and confined against my will by a bunch of accused murderers. I mean, can you imagine? I'm sitting in that bull pen knowing I was not supposed to be in there and I was sitting in that jail with real murderers and criminals which I was neither. There were 17 men including myself facing murder charges that day.

Some of these guys had already been to prison before and that made it even more difficult and uncomfortable for me. The whole time though, I couldn't just stay focused on my situation because I was also concerned about LJ because LJ wasn't what we would consider a big strong dude. He was skinny and I knew that was an automatic disadvantage for him so I remained concerned about him. I called out to him and asked him did he say anything. He said that he didn't say anything and asked me if I said anything. I told him that they had tricked me into giving a confession because they had told me that he had also confessed. After I said that, the next thing I heard was a bunch of inmates laughing. Then one of the inmates in an adjacent cell said to me, "young blood, I know you didn't make a statement". I repeated what I said to LJ which was that they tricked me. They started laughing again.

I sat there and started to think about what had transpired a few hours earlier. I mean, it started to really hit me at that point that the lieutenant who questioned me deliberately set the tape at Sherry's confession. I could have at that point just denied everything that she said. They really didn't have anything at that point to charge me with other than hearsay. I remember just being so numb listening to the tape and hearing my sister sing like a canary telling everything that had happened except that in every part of the story where she was guilty, she put my name in her place. I guess in my mindset at that time, I just felt I had to confess to defend my own honor at that point because I couldn't comprehend what would make her throw me under the bus like that. In my mind,

I was thinking, Oh hell no, You are not fixing to pin this crap on me so I am about to tell them what really happened. Knowing what I know now, I wish I had kept my damned mouth shut but I was young and so naive and just wanted to defend and protect my honor.

The whole time while I was reflecting back on everything, the inmates were still laughing and making mockery of my naive mistake that a more polished individual wouldn't have made. Then suddenly the laughter stopped. Things remained quiet the rest of that night. I just laid there peering into the ceiling trying to understand the magnitude of what was happening to me and what was going to happen next. Eventually I ended up falling asleep. It was the most uncomfortable sleep I had ever had up til that point. There I was on a hard bed that was too small for my 6'2 frame. I was cold and I think the only thing that kept me warm was the heat from my anger, grief, fear and sense of betrayal that was boiling throughout my blood.

Finally daybreak came and it was time to eat breakfast. I didn't eat anything at that time because I was so stressed out. After everyone else ate, we went back into our respective cells. I waited and waited each day wishing for that miracle to happen so I could finally go home. Each day seemed longer than the day before. It took them 42 days to arraign me. Finally that day came. The deputy on duty in the cell block came and said, " Wilson, Moore you are going to be arraigned today, get ready for court." After about an hour later they came to take us to court. As they opened the cell doors I caught a quick glance at LJ and could tell that he was scared. I wanted to let him know things were going to work out when the truth came out but I couldn't say anything to him. They led us through a tunnel to get to the court room. There were 12 other prisoners being led to the courthouse along with us.

They took me to a holding room that led to the

courtroom. I sat there waiting for a little while and then the deputy came up to me and told me that I had an attorney waiting to see me. You see, mama had hired an attorney for me after having put up her house as collateral for my attorney fees. I had about 40,000 stashed away that I had made from selling weed which was also used to help pay the attorney. Hey, I didn't say I was a saint. I'm just not a murderer. The attorney my mom hired was an Italian looking fellow. The deputies escorted me to a private room to talk with my new attorney.

He extended out his hand and introduced himself. He told me his name was David McDonald and that he was there to represent me. The first thing I wanted to know was what were my chances of getting out of this mess before it went to a trial? Then he said to me that there is a remote possibility that I could get out on a bond. He told me that he would try to ask for a bond hearing but for that moment, he wanted to deal with the arraignment process. He told me he wanted me to go in there and plead not guilty. He said that the judge would be asking me some questions but I was to remain firm and say not guilty. Then we got up and headed into the courtroom but through separate corridors. The deputies escorted me into the courtroom.

I sat in my seat overwhelmed with uncertainty. I just wanted this process to hurry up so I could get out of there and get back to my girl Tracy and my family. Then the Judge sat down on the bench and called out my name. "Maurice Moore", he said. I stood up and as instructed by the deputy, I looked directly at the Judge. Although I was standing there physically, it felt as though my mind was off in some other dimension. The charges against me were read and the main thing I heard was the last statement by the judge which was how do you plead? With strong confidence and conviction I said with an emphatic voice; "not guilty."

The judge then explained the severity of the charges and then set a court date for one month later for the preliminary hearing. I was then allowed to have a brief talk with my attorney who at that point was basically doing all he could to to try to help me keep hope alive. I wanted that conversation to last as long as possible to keep from having to go back to my cell so I kept thinking of questions to ask him. Unfortunately I ran out of things to ask and so they led me back to my cell and again, I saw LJ being led back to his as well. He had just finished up with his arraignment too. Once I got settled in my cell, I heard a loud voice a few cells down from where I was. Bay Bay, Bay Bay. I was like, wait a minute, hold up! Is that Sherry? Then I heard it again. Bay Bay, Bay Bay, the voice shouted.

I knew it was my sister even though part of me didn't want to believe it. Apparently she had been moved to the county jail to also be arraigned after having given her confession. I shouted out her name twice and she asked me where was I at? I said, "I'm down here, I'm down here." She told me not to say anything and not to worry about nothing because she was going to take care of everything. I said alright. At that point a strong sense of calm and confidence started to dominate my spirit. I felt hopeful that my sister would set the record straight and soon I would be out of the mess I was in. A few hours later I received another visit from my newly acquired attorney. He informed me that LJ had hired himself an attorney. I asked him would I be able to get a bond. He said that the first thing he was going to do was to file a motion to have my confession suppressed. I assured him that I only made a statement because I was scared after hearing what my sister said on the tape. I reverted back to my question though because I was eager to hear an answer. What were the chances of me getting a bond hearing because I wanted out of that predicament and I wanted to be out as soon as possible.

He didn't directly provide an answer to my question.

Instead, what he said was that he would do his best to get my statement suppressed because it was coerced and hopefully because of that fact, the judge may issue a bond. He told me no matter what, that he was going to fight as hard as he could for me. He assured me that he understood the pain this was causing my mother. He told me that he had to hold her up in court to keep her from passing out. He told me that he assured my mother that he would do all he could to get me home. That gave me a little sense of calm and resolve. I felt that at least I had someone in my corner who was sensitive enough about the situation to hug my mother and tell her it is going to be ok. That meant the world to me. His confidence was making a great impression on me which in turn caused me to have strong faith in his abilities. He told me that he would make sure that he would frequently come back to see me to keep me informed as to the status of my case and what strategies he would be using in court to defend me. He shook my hand and bid me farewell. Then the deputy came and got me and took me back to my cell.

As I walked to my cell I was feeling many emotions. My emotions were giving me mixed signals because on one hand, I felt a sense of confidence after hearing what my attorney had just told me. On the other hand, I knew that my fate was still in the hands of a judge so my confidence was in conflict with the concern over the reality of my situation. To top it off, I was hungry too. I hadn't eaten anything ever since I had been arrested so I felt famished. The unfortunate thing was that they have a regulated time for eating so I just had to be patient and wait until chow time. I just kept holding my stomach as I was being escorted back to my cell. A few days had passed before I finally saw LJ again out in the yard. I went up to him and said to him, "man, I thought you said that you didn't make a statement". He said that he didn't make a statement. I told him that was not what my attorney told me and that I believed that my attorney had no reason to lie to me and was therefore telling me the truth. He then said to me, "I didn't say anything man, I didn't say anything". I told him that either he was lying or my attorney was lying.

Now, I could tell that the conversation was irritating him and it was irritating me even more so. LJ said, "You'll see, You'll see, I am going to help you. I am going to let them know you didn't do anything. I just looked directly at him and gave him a cold stare. In my mind I felt so betrayed. I mean, here was someone who was once a childhood friend and more like a brother to me but now he had become an enemy. I started feeling that LJ was going to be the weak link in the case and I began to feel that my allegiance must be with my sister. After he said, "You'll see, I said, yea, we'll see and then I asked the guard to take me back to my cell because at that moment I was so pissed off at LJ to the point that I didn't even want to look at him anymore.

When I got back to my cell, I just laid on my rock hard bed overtaken by an anger and grief that was laced with pessimism. That proverbial sense of hope that my attorney had given me seemed to dwarf into the shadows being blocked by the dominating reality of betrayal that my friend LJ and my own flesh and blood sister had committed against me. I tried my best to block out what I was feeling while attempting to reclaim that grip on what was honestly a small glimmer of hope that I was going to get out of this legal jam with relative ease. I hoped exoneration would come with relative ease because I knew I didn't kill no body. Unfortunately however, throughout the night all I could think about was the betrayal. I mean, how could my childhood friend turn on me?

Why would he play me like that, I kept asking myself over and over again? I mean, why would he treat me like that when I was always the one person he could always turn to in his desperate times of need. On top of all that, I was always his protector growing up. If anyone had a beef with him, they had a beef with me. That is how I was concerning my camaraderie with him but there I was laying on a bed that in my mind felt probably just as hard as the bed that the cartoon character Fred Flintstone from the stone age slept in. I laid there feeling betrayed by someone who was supposed to be my ace. Back and forth I kept thinking about his and Sherry's betrayal. Although I was highly pissed off at Sherry for her betrayal too, I kept rationalizing to myself that because she said she would fix everything, I had to give her a pass and overlook what she had done but, as for LJ, I felt I had every right to be angry and feel betrayed. Even as fatigue began to take over my body, as I began to fall asleep, this whole nightmare still was in the forefront of my mind assailing me as I dozed off to sleep. I remained in that frame of mind for weeks on end.

My attorney came a week before the preliminary hearing and told me that my chances of beating this case were slim to none. He stated that even though the evidence was circumstantial, it would be enough to send me away for life simply because he knew something that I didn't know at that time which was the fact that my sister and LJ had taken a plea deal in exchange for giving testimony against me. The betrayal was overwhelming me and all hope that had been fading was completely gone. Then it came time for the preliminary hearing. My attorney went separately into a room to meet with the Prosecutor. He came back to the waiting room where I sat and informed me of the deal they were willing to offer me. Now keep in mind that at that age, I had absolutely no kind of understanding about how the law works or court procedure or even about what my rights were. Reluctantly, I accepted the plea deal. First degree Murder came with an automatic life sentence without the possibility of parole. That is what I was facing.

The Prosecutor came in the room with the paperwork to sign and informed me that Sherry and LJ were offered a plea to which they both had taken. My attorney had advised me that the plea deal was my best option by convincing me that 25 years to life with parole possibility sounded much better than life without the possibility of parole. So I took the deal and signed the waiver rather than facing court but I still had to be formally arraigned. Once again, without understanding anything about the law, I gave up my right to have a speedy trial by signing that waiver and now that I know so much more about the law, I probably would have handled things a little bit differently. Then the deputy asked me if I would like to participate in the formal process to bound me over into custody in the courtroom to which I said no. I was being influenced by the mockery the inmates threw at me weeks earlier and figured that I was doing the right thing this time by refusing to participate in any proceedings. Besides, I did not want to watch them bask in any more glory at my expense.

Chapter 5
Prison The Early Years

Shortly after taking a plea deal of First Degree Murder, I was shipped out of the Genesee county jail and sent to a Corrections Receiving Facility in Ionia, Michigan. This was the prison where new prisoners in Michigan in a certain region were sent to first to be processed into the system. The atmosphere in the holding receiving area was so much more different than the county jail in Flint, Michigan. I learned right away why they called that facility "Gladiator School." This place was indeed a teaching ground for what to expect in prison life and how to act accordingly. If you made it through Gladiator School, you could make it in any other prison facility.

I definitely had to learn the ropes and learn them quick because upon entry into that facility, I had to immediately make a choice concerning how I was to be perceived by everyone else from that point forward. I wondered, am I supposed to be the big brute everyone fears? Am I supposed to be the mellow guy that everyone would think is soft? Am I supposed to act tough or just be myself and be that fun loving goofy guy I've always been? Would being myself be more harmful to me than trying to flex my muscle in a jungle amongst real murderers and serial killers? I really didn't have much time to decide because no sooner than after I walked through the corridor of the facility, gladiator class began and I had to become an alert student.

Although on the surface, I had to show a strong face, inside I was terrified of the unknown but prepared to deal with whatever this new life was about to throw at me. As I prepared to force my feet to walk toward that door to enter the facility, I remember talking to myself as I gave myself encouragement pep talks. Ok, Ok, this is it bruh, here we go. Just be ready for anything and anybody. I'm not looking for no trouble but I'm not about to become somebody else bitch. I'm not about to take no shit off of nobody.

I stayed on guard constantly observing every little detail of my surroundings and the people around me and taking mental notes. I tried not to wear the see through masks of worry, fear, over exaggerated toughness, over confidence or paranoia but I think at times, my face showed evidence that I was going through all of these thoughts and emotions. To be honest, I was an emotional wreck but had to do everything in my power to conceal what my face kept wanting to reveal. So out came that phony smile, that face of bravado, that face of toughness. I had to show that glaring don't even think about trying to fuck with me face to send a message to any and everyone who would even think about trying me.

The administrators immediately upon entry, talked to us like we were nothing and treated us like we were nothing. They didn't even know if we were guilty of the crimes we were there for or if we were innocent and they didn't care. In their minds, everyone was a wicked criminal and everyone was treated with disrespect. After forcing my unwilling feet to walk into that facility, all I saw at the receiving entrance were big burly white men who were the security guards. It seemed like they had deliberately picked them to intimidate the newcomers. The Newcomers were called fish. We were the new fish coming in and those white guards were there to intimidate us. At that time, I couldn't imagine what to expect next.

Never did I imagine that years later I would have witnessed so many grown men crying. So many men just so happy to see sunlight and so many other things we take for granted. I wasn't even there a full hour and I witnessed several inmates being taken to the infirmary for having been injured from stab wounds. It was around Thanksgiving time when I first arrived at Ionia facility. I remember saying to myself, ain't nobody stabbing me. I looked over at one of the attendants handling one of the inmates who had been stabbed and asked her if that man was going to make it? She told me that he was not going to make it and also stated that this happens all the time. She said he will probably be dead before he arrives at the hospital.

What was disturbing about her demeanor is that she didn't seem to have any empathy or compassion in her voice about that man or the situation. It was as if she had developed an immunity to her own spirit. I later found out that she was actually a good person but that she had become so numb with her feelings and reaction to these stabbings because they were daily occurrences as a norm in that world. After she had told me that the man wasn't going to make it, I said to her, this is not going to be my life. They ended up assigning me and LJ to the same floor. This facility has two big blocks. Each block has five minor blocks within it and the prison was shaped like an L . It houses 2000 men. They put 200 men in each level.

I looked around at the area and thought about all of the possible crimes these men were in that prison for. I knew I was in for a long battle for my survival. I couldn't have imagined what things I would experience in the years ahead which still impact my life today. I endured all of that while knowing without doubt I didn't kill Mr. Wellington. After experiencing what I went through in prison, I just feel that it is extremely important that everyone knows exactly what happens in there before people post judgments against convicted felons. Many people who have been accused of a crime and convicted may not be guilty. Juries do make mistakes. In my case, as I have stated to you before, my lawyer basically tricked me into believing that I did not stand a chance against a jury trial and convinced me that my best chance of seeing freedom ever again was to take a plea bargain.

Finally, I was taken to my cell. We were given two sheets, a thin blanket, a pillow case, a small tube of tooth paste and a small toothbrush. The blanket was almost as thin as the sheet and this became an indicator to me of what was to come.

Later on they called us out to get our quarter masters which are the blue, state issued prison uniforms. Because I was such a huge man, I didn't hear anyone make any sexual advances toward me, any cat calls or anything like that. But I did hear them doing so toward LJ and I felt so bad for him. It just so happened that LJ was placed in the furthest cell away from me. He was on the very last room on one end and I was placed in the very last post on my end. Although we were on opposite sides of the complex, I just felt compelled to look out for him.

Then I arrived at my cell as the guard was escorting me to it. I looked around trying to catch a quick glance inside the cell to see if there were ay roaches because I heard that this particular facility was infested with roaches. Luckily, I didn't see any. The room did however look so filthy as if it had not been cleaned in years. At that moment I turned towards the guard. He looked at me and said, "welcome to your new home". I looked directly into his eyes with strong conviction and said, this ain't my home. This ain't going to never be my home. This ain't nobody's home. Then he ushered me into my cell saying go on into your cell. Once I got into the cell, for the first time during this whole ordeal, I felt angry. My anger wasn't against my sister Sherry, not against LJ and not against the system. I was angry at that guard for trying to antagonize me.

When those bars closed, my whole body tensed up. I mean, I don't think up to the point I had never felt so angry. This includes the anger I felt when I heard my sister blatantly lie on me on that confession tape. The anger I felt then pales in comparison to that moment when the officer shoved me into that cell. It felt as though this man was rubbing it in my face. He didn't know if I was guilty or innocent of the crime I was in there for and he didn't care and I guess that's what pissed me off the most. When that cell closed and I heard the sound... Clank..it finally hit me. That reality finally started to set in that I'm not going to sleep in my own bed outside of the prison walls probably for a long time.

Most of the guys I talked to about their first experience when they were forced into their cell for the first time all basically said the same thing. The reality and magnitude of what is about to happen for the next years of your life start to come into full view. That cell became my new reality. I was no longer in that protective sense of denial. Before that moment, I had been in denial about everything. When the police first came to my house to arrest me and LJ, I was in denial. When they transported me to the police station, I was still in denial. When they took me to interrogation, I was still in denial. When they told me they were charging me with murder, I was yet still in denial. None of that stuff was affecting me at those points because I was so numb with disbelief. I didn't even feel it when the judge sentenced me. But as soon as those bars closed, it suddenly hit me like a tsunami. As long as I exist on earth, I will never forget that sound. CLANK! ..

I fight to hold back tears right now as I am getting highly emotional trying to relive that moment as I try to convey my story to you. It is so overwhelming because it hit me really hard, I mean real hard. As I am telling this story to you right now, I'm having to pause and pull myself together. Can you imagine iron bars closing on you locking you in a prison cell for a crime you know you did not commit? You hear that clanking sound and fear that you quite possibly will never see outside of a prison ever again. At that moment, to add insult to what was already the most devastating injury my spirit had ever faced, that officer gave me another look as if to say, "you're so dumb". I knew and understood what that look meant but I was determined to let my will prevail over his mockery and I was determined that someday I would get the last laugh and walk out of there a free man. I kept saying to myself , this is not my home. I looked around that cell and I didn't want to even sit on that nasty bed.

They always claimed that Janitors come and clean the cells to prepare them for the new arrivals but my cell was not cleaned at all. It was filthy. I had seen hog pins that looked and smelled better than my cell. I reaffirmed myself yet again saying: this ain't my home. I had to stay in that cell until 6:00 that next morning. Even though the clanking sound caused me to realize the magnitude of what was happening to me, I still kept a lingering sense of denial within me. You see, they gave us a bed roll consisting of the things we would need for sleep and personal hygiene.

I had not even unraveled my bed roll bundle because I kept thinking someone was going to call me out of my cell and tell me that this has all been a mistake and that I was free. I was so sure that this was just a bad dream or that they made a mistake in bringing me to prison. I slept however, with my prison blue uniform on but still anticipating I was going home in the morning. As I stated before though, the blanket they gave me anyway was almost as thin as the sheet they gave me. The pillows were so flat they felt like they folded two sheets and sewed them together and said that's your pillow. I remember glancing over at that bed and once again I had to remind myself: this ain't my home.

I laid there staring at the dark walls and at the light from the galley outside of my cell as it was glowing onto part of the wall. I was thinking about how could I devise a plan to get out of here. I knew nothing about the prison so escape was not even a topic of thought for me. I began thinking to myself saying: maybe I can say something to the warden to convince him that I'm innocent and that I'm not supposed to be in here. I drove myself crazy throughout that night and into the early morning trying to think of ways to get out of there. I was not trying to socialize with anybody, was not trying to feel out the prison, not trying to see who I knew up in there either. I wasn't thinking about a shower, clothes anything resembling hygiene.

My mind was fixated on trying to figure out how was I going to get the hell up out of there because both me and God knew I was not supposed to be there. I kept thinking about that prison guard saying welcome to your new home. I just had to get out of there. That night and into that morning, I didn't cry and even if I wanted to, I was so determined to get out of there that I didn't have time to cry. Thinking thoughts of how was I going to get out of there were the only thoughts I wanted to think. Nothing else mattered to me. I wanted my freedom. I wanted my life back and somehow, someway, I was determined that I was going to get what I wanted.

The next morning I made that long walk to the chow hall. The walk was not only a long walk but it was a bitter cold walk. You see, they will tell you publicly that prison is a place for rehabilitation and punishment but it is mostly a place for punishment. Keeping the facility as cold as possible during the winter months is a tactic they use against the prisoners to break their spirits and their will. They strategically placed the chow hall at the farthest distance away from the cell blocks to force us to take that long cold walk. Nonetheless, I begrudgingly made that long frigid walk because I knew that was going to be one of the few times I could get out from under that filthy cell. Finally I made it into the chow hall.

Once I got in there, I began to look around and saw a few people from Flint where I grew up. It was kind of a helpful relief to see some familiar faces. That helped me deal with prison life a little more better through the years. As I walked in there, there were two ways you could go to get in the lines for your food. You could either go to the left or go to the right but either way you choose, there was going to be a long line. As I waited in line, I went into observation mode. I was looking at everything within proximity of my vision. I was looking for certain mannerisms and characteristics of everyone so I could kind of get an assessment of who I was going to be dealing with in the future quite possibly.

At that same time though, I was wearing an internal smile because of the people I did recognize. I remember saying to myself: I know him, and him, and oh yeah I definitely know that dude. Some of them noticed I was noticing them. One in particular was one of the Pearson brothers, a family I knew locally from Flint. He definitely saw me and gave that nodding heads up motion as if to say what's up. I also saw another dude named Darren. He had just recently killed someone in December. He approached me and said; "hey man, how's your family, how's everybody doing"? After I had told him that everyone in my family was doing ok and since I had already known why he was in prison, I decided to ask him if everyone up in there was in prison for the same thing? I mean, is everyone up in here like this? He said, like what? I said innocent, like me, I'm innocent. I didn't kill nobody. He said, "man everybody is innocent". He then said, " don't tell nobody you did that". When he had said that statement, I didn't initially understand it.

It was years later that I finally comprehended what he was trying to say. Needless to say, in that moment, he continued to give me knowledge of what to expect and how to survive up in that environment. He told me that I had to get myself a shank. I said, for what? He then said,"everybody got one and you're gonna need it because at any given time you could get shanked and you would rather have your gun with you rather than to not have one". I said, a gun? He said, "yeah, that is what a shank is called up in here." I told him that he's going to have to get me one then. So he told me that he would get me a hawk and a shank. A hawk is a mirror that prisoners stick outside of there cell to see who is coming toward their cell. Its a first line defense against any would be attacker. So a shank and a hawk were essential to survival.

What is so amazing about that experience is that I immediately noticed how clever the inmates were. In that type of environment, you had to improvise on almost any and everything. From protecting yourself to preserving food for a later date, they basically had everything down to a science. I will elaborate more on some of the food preservation techniques later. Although I did want the hawk and shank, I never was the type of person to just use a weapon on anyone. Growing up, I was always a big kid and everyone respected my bigness to the extent that nobody wanted to challenge me to fight because they feared they would get the beat-down. I didn't go walking around looking for trouble acting like a bully as I stated earlier but my big body frame gave younger cats that type of impression.

I was a gentle giant and I still am to this day. I went ahead and decided that maybe I should get both of them just in case something ever went down. So I said to Darren, man when can you get that for me. He said, "I can get it for you now". Then we started to leave from the chow hall to go get the stuff. While we were walking, he said to me, "man, I hate that you are in here though". At that time, I wasn't aware of that fact that he had previously been in there for 7 years.

I later found out that Darren was gay. One of his friends walked up to me and asked, "are you Darren's homeboy"? I said yeah. He then said, "he is trying to fuck you". I looked at him and asked, what do you mean, mess me up for what? He said, "naw man, he want your butt". I looked at him and said man, ain't nobody doing nothing like that to me. I don't swing that way and I don't appreciate you talking to me like that. Then he looked at me and said, " let me tell yo little young dumb ass something, I was just trying to tell your ass that your homeboy is a predator and he don't care nothing about yo ass. He don't care whether you are his friend, his brother or whether you swing that way or not. He wanna fuck you". I looked at him knowing that where I come from, either you are going to whoop my ass or I'm going to whoop yours and so I said, hey, look here man, I don't know your name but ain't nobody fucking me and I done already told you that I don't swing that way.

That was the first incident where I had to stand my ground. It came back to bite me later on. I later found out also that Darren had a lot of pull up in the prison. That very next day, Darren had already delivered the shank and the hawk with an attached note saying that I will see you tomorrow. After I read the note, I made up my cot and I said to my cellmate, where do you keep your shank? He replied, "what kind of dumb mother fuckin question is that?" Keep in mind that I had no idea about prison life and so I was young and naive about the rules of the game so to speak.

Then he said, I ain't going to tell you man, I don't know you. I'm not going to tell you where I keep my knife at so you can tell the police. And don't you tell nobody where you keep your knife at either. You can get a case for that." I said, a case, what is a case? He said, "another charge on top of your sentence". I said, Oh. I was just going to stick mine under my mattress while not knowing that they do shakedowns and look under the mattress. I was glad he told me that because I could have gotten my naive self into serious trouble even though I was mad at him for the disrespectful way he said it. You see, in prison life, you have to command for yourself a level of respect because if you show any kind of sign of weakness, it will be exploited and people will think you are soft or a wimp. I let him slide however with the disrespect but I made a mental note to myself that someday I might have to see that guy again so I had better be prepared.

There is a basic understanding in prison that when a person says to you, all is well, then you had better be watching your back. You can't let a guy walk away from you telling you that all is well because all is well did not mean that everything is ok or everything is good. All is well or when they say something like "we good" really means be aware of the fact that later when you least expect it, I'm going to shank your ass." You automatically knew that whenever someone said to you after a confrontation, "all is well, then you had better have your shank with you at all times because they were coming after you or if they were powerful enough, meaning that they were a king pin of some sort, they were going to send somebody else after you. All of these little pieces of knowledge I was learning were critical pieces I needed to know in order to survive up in there. I was only 19 and although I learned from the streets how to survive by being with my big sister all the time, that street life was not enough to prepare me for prison so to speak because the world in prison is a whole other world than how it is outside those iron bars and brick walls and barbed wire.

I started to think about what he had said to me about getting caught with a shank and how more time could be added to my prison sentence. I didn't want no more time added and I wasn't even remotely thinking about killing anyone and so I threw the shank away. And the dude who gave it to me said, "man is you dumb?" I said to him, "man, I ain't stabbing nobody. I told him, I don't understand none of y'all for stabbing nobody. Man, I don't know whats wrong with you all. Everyone was out there in the yard with us when I said what I said. They were either playing cards, or exercising even though it was cold out there. I said it loud enough for all of them to hear me. I don't understand none of y'all for stabbing no body. Then he said to me, "man you better shut up."

I went back to my cell after our yard time was over and I said to myself,' I'm not walking with a bunch of people and I'm not taking no shower with a bunch of men. I'm going to the shower with my clothes on fully dressed. Boy was I wrong. The next morning I got a really rude awakening. I had to walk down the gallery wearing only my towel feeling fully exposed. Not only did we have to walk down our gallery but we had to walk past the guards station. What made it a little more tolerable was the fact that the floors were relatively clean.

As time passed, I began to develop relationships with certain guards who would then let me take a little extra longer showers. I can tell you this much about those showers. You learned to appreciate the small things such as warm water and soap. Every second I was away from my cell and in that warm shower in a sense felt like the only type of heavenly experience I'd ever get to feel in that place. Solidarity away from all that was oppressing my spirit. You, can't imagine how much of a treasured experience each shower became and these are things we all take for granted when we have our freedom. Sometimes we developed such business relationships with certain guard to the point where we could offer to pay them about 200 dollars to sneak and unlock a door in the visitation room so that we could sneak our girlfriends in there and have sex. We weren't even supposed to interact with the guards but rules and regulations can never overpower the inevitable nature of good personalities befriending each other.

There were only a select few who would be willing to do it and you basically had to gain each others trust over time and build a relationship that came with mutual understanding. They knew not to cross you and you dared not to cross them because you needed them more than they needed you. We knew every man has a price and money was their weakness which we happily took advantage of. All they had to do was leave the door unlocked and turn a blind eye for about 15-20 quick minutes and they made a quick 200 dollars. They would go on lunch break while we handled our business but required that they get the money in their hands first.

Sometimes we would luck up and as one of the other inmates who had already paid for sex was going out of the room and the guard was not looking, we would sneak in behind that couple who were coming out and we would end up having the room free of charge. Then, there were the female guards. There were plenty of them to go around. Some of us were lucky enough to have any one of those women guards they wanted. My homeboy who I met at another facility named Salih was the one person in there who could have any of those women but he chose to stay steadfast in his Islamic faith and remained celibate. Hey, I'm not knocking him but the attitude of most men in there was that if you are lucky enough to get it, then you better get it. That wasn't the case with Salih. He turned down every chick and I admired him for sticking to his convictions no matter what.

At first I thought he was just a square dude and that was before I was introduced to Islam and before I knew he was even a Muslim. I just thought the dude was weird for turning down all of those opportunities to have sex with all those women prison guards who wanted him. I remember asking him, why he wouldn't get with those women who keep trying to hook up with him? I couldn't understand why this man wanted to pray all the time and not be interested in women who were interested in him. I knew for sure that he was not gay and so I couldn't understand why he chose celibacy over sexual pleasure that was practically being thrown at him. There were some beautiful women guards up in there and most of them wanted him but he just wasn't trying to break his practice of celibacy. He certainly did not let being in prison alter his beliefs or his commitment to his religion and the principles of Islam.

Looking back now as I am free, I often ask myself, would I do things differently and practice celibacy too which would make me much like my brother Salih? I can't honestly answer with a definitive yes or no because here is how I look at it. I was taken unjustly away from society and stripped of my freedom. Sex is part of the human experience and I was being denied of that basic human right or privilege against my will and all because of a murder which I did not commit. So, when the opportunity came to get that human pleasure, I felt I was well within my human right to experience it. I didn't know if I was ever going to see outside of those prison walls ever again. At least in my brother Salih case, he had a possible out date because he was serving a 15 year sentence. I was serving 25 years to life and that made me feel my chances of getting out someday was basically at the mercy of a parole board so I felt that if and when I had a chance to be with a woman up in there, I was going to take it. I will elaborate more on how I first met Salih and how we ended up becoming best friends later on. In the meantime, I want to share with you all how my naive thinking got me in trouble the very first time I took a shower at the prison.

I was so naive and had no clue about the rules of showering because nobody had told me. So I took this long walk down the corridor to go and take my shower. I didn't know that we were only supposed to get 5 minutes in the shower and so I took my time getting myself prepared for my shower. Once I finally hopped into the shower and lathered my body up with soap, the guard called out my name saying " Moore, time to get out of the shower". I said, ok, I'm about to get out in a few minutes, I just need to rinse the soap off. The guard said, "no, out of the shower now". I asked, can't I just rinse the soap off? I heard all the other people in the shower laughing at me. The guard repeated his command but I kept trying to hurry up and rinse off as much water as I could. Then all of a sudden some big burly guards came rushing into the shower and grabbed me out of the shower while I was still naked with soap all over my body.

As they were taking me out of the shower, I heard the other prisoners laughing at me saying, "dumb ass, they got his dumb ass." They did not take me to any solitary confinement. Instead, they stood me right in front of the guard station in the window and gave me a lecture telling me that whenever they give me a command to do something, that I had better do it right away or I would be charged with a DDO which means disobeying a direct order. Once I made it back to my cell, I thought to myself, man, I better learn these laws up in here because I'm not trying to be in here making trouble for myself or nothing.

Now initially when I first got to prison, they allowed us to wear civilian gear from outside and my family would bring me clothes to wear. That made me feel a little better about my situation. You can't imagine how something as simple as a shirt and a pair of designer jeans and a nice pair of shoes can have a huge impact of your mental state of being while being locked up behind iron bars. Those pieces of clothing gave me some sense of connection back to the world I had just come from. Those items were the only things I had some sort of power and control over because the prison system had control over my life, my time, when I ate, whether I got medicine when I was sick and every aspect of my existence.

Property in prison boosted or lowered your stature in prison. You were classified into certain levels of prominence or lack of prominence based on the type of property you owned such as a TV or a pair of Air Jordan athletic shoes. Receiving a letter from outside also influenced your standing in there as well. Tons of letters meant that you were loved by family and friends and it meant that you were most likely going to get some money or some visits. Prisoners paid close attention to those small details about each individual person and as a consequence, we had to be careful even about our clothing.

Whenever I got new clothes, I always felt like people were watching me. Naturally, this caused me to have to watch them too. There is no such thing as being nosy in prison. Everybody was always watching everybody and we all knew that was normal. As a result of this unwritten behavioral understanding, I noticed that I was being stalked by certain individuals. One time, I received some clothes on a Tuesday and by Wednesday

I had been robbed of those clothing items. I was so saddened beyond measure because those clothing items were the only thing I had that gave me a sense of pride and connection to the outside and to my family. I went to the yard and everyone was out there on the yard except this one janitor porter. I looked around on the yard and I didn't see anyone wearing my clothes. Then that next day in the morning, I went to the chow hall and what I saw looked like that scene from the movie "COMING TO AMERICA" when Akeem and Semi's clothing was stolen and they came outside and saw all of the people of the community wearing their belongings. I saw a guy with my coat on, and I saw a guy with my Eddie Bauer jacket on. I saw men wearing my sweat hoodies. So many people were wearing my clothing that next morning after having been robbed.

Still naive to the rules of prison life, I went to confront them. I walked up to one of them and said, man, how did you get my shoes. He just looked at me and laughed. Then he said, "what you see up in here, you don't see and what you hear you don't hear so stop asking questions". The code of prison world is that you never tell on nobody or that may cost you your life. That very next day I saw more guys walking around wearing my clothes. There were so many that it took me a minute to pin point which one of them I wanted to walk up to and confront. Finally I built up enough nerve and walked up to one of them and asked him where did he get those clothes. He told me that he had purchased them from one of the men who was on my cell block. It just so happened to be that same man who I talked to the day before who had told me that what you see in prison, you don't see and what you hear, you don't hear. I was so pissed off at that moment. I knew I had to confront him.

I had gotten hold of another shank and I had planned to bring it with me to confront him because I was so angry that my stuff was taken from me and also because of the most important factor of all. When you make no response when an

71

inmate does something to you or takes something from you then word spreads rapidly throughout the prison that you are a soft person and then every predator will try to test you with bullying or, try to sexually assault you or even steal from you again. I felt I had to make an example out of this guy to protect myself and my reputation but when that time came, he was already ready and expecting me. He was also carrying a shank and his was much bigger than mine. It was about the size of my arm in length and he immediately pulled it out and said, "listen to this boy, you are our property now. You don't own nothing. You don't even own your own life and if you tell, we're going to kill you. Even though he had the upper hand, I had my hand on my shank ready to slice his head off had he tried anything.

Make no mistake however, even though I didn't physically do any bodily harm to him, lets just say, I had an I am not going to let nobody walk over me attitude and I was going to find a way to get him back even if it meant turning his enemies against him and letting them get justice for me without even realizing it. I had made a vow not to stab nobody up in there and that such violent behavior never defined my life and wasn't going to define it just because I had to share space with ruthless criminals and murders. I was not a criminal and certainly not a murderer and I wasn't going to let prison life change me into one either. I was determined to be who I was before they placed those shackles on me. I wasn't going to be no homosexual and I wasn't going to kill nobody. Those clothes were not worth me losing my life over and jeopardizing my freedom or my intended reward in the hereafter in paradise which is all I ever hope for. I am not a murderer and I wanted to be a proof to the rest of the prisoners that prison can't convert me into a murderer either. I didn't care if everyone viewed me afterward as too soft or too nice. It didn't matter to me because that prison life was not mine. I was in prison but I never ever accepted it as my home.

The following week after that incident, as a consequence of my not wanting to confront that dude who initially stole all of my stuff, I ended up being involved in my first fight. Leading up to that fight, I had been harassed by many of the guys and called many derogatory names. One person who was wearing my clothing had the audacity to ask me how to clean my damned coat which he was wearing. Can you believe that? He was wearing my shit and asking me how to clean it. Man, let me tell you. I was highly pissed off. I looked at him with an angry glare and noticed that he had his fists clinched waiting for me to make a move against him. I had already been inflamed with rage because of the fact that my clothes had been stolen and there I was standing directly in front of one of the people who was wearing my clothing and he was making a mockery of me in front of everyone by having the nerve to ask me how to clean my own shit.

I was boiled with anger and I punched him in his face and then followed it up with a series of blows to prevent him from having a chance to react and mount a defense. He fell to the ground as I continued my onslaught. I tried to snatch my coat off of him that he was wearing. That's when the guards came rushing in and broke us apart. I ended up doing 14 days in solitary confinement. When I was finally released from solitary confinement, I was shown a greater amount of respect from my fellow inmates. Although I was determined not to kill anyone, I definitely needed to send that message to everyone so they could understand that I am not a punk they can just do what they want to do to and expect no consequence. Let's just say that from that point on, everybody knew not to fuck with me.

I started becoming stressed at everything I was going through up in there trying to merely survive in a jungle among wild human animals. I needed a distraction and had hoped I could get some visits from whomever just to get out of that cell and away from that environment. I filed an appeal hoping to get my sentence overturned due to the fact my statements to the police were taken without me having an attorney present and for many other factors. That became a waiting game because the courts were so backlogged with so many other cases. It forced me to have patience. I took up welding and small engine assembly and other courses to occupy my time. I even took courses to earn my GED. During that time, I started getting more frequent visits from my girlfriend Tracy.

Each time she came I was elated but sorrowful because I knew that eventually the visit would have to end and I wouldn't see her for a few weeks or months. Nonetheless, I tried to make the best of every moment. My brother Ralph and my sister Janice began to come up more often as well and that helped distract me from thinking about my clothes. They eventually brought me more clothing and this time, I learned my lesson and protected my stuff much better. I needed more clothes anyway because I had outgrown some of that stuff and was getting bigger by the minute it seemed. I was getting bigger because I could put away some food like a beast. My family started sending me money to help support my eating frenzy.

I had seen so many men go hungry every day in there because they weren't fortunate enough to have family who could afford to send them money and this went on the whole time throughout my tenure in prison. I watched how the prison system would throw away all of that extra food after our chow time rather than giving those who were possibly still hungry an opportunity to eat a little more. Instead, they chose to throw all of that food into the garbage. I remember how many guys would be so creative that they would save two pieces of bread from the previous meal, then save their peanut butter from lunch and make a sandwich out of that for later on whenever they became hungry again. We had to do what we had to do up in there. It wasn't just about survival of the fittest in prison life. It was about survival period by any means necessary regardless of what strengths you had. Everyone was resilient in their will to live and survive and especially for the ones who had hope that someday they would come home.

Even when it came to finding ways to support cigarette habits, prisoners were creative in their ways to get what they wanted and often needed. There was no shortage of cigarettes because there was always somebody on the outside who was a direct connection to a supplier. The same applies to what was considered contraband. Eventually they outlawed cigarettes too but they found ways to get around that. Most of the time they would put cologne on tissue paper and wave it around in the room to mask the smell. Other times, they would put baby powder into the air and that masked the smell as well. Additionally, we would open up our vents which would also help remove the scent.

Serving time in prison is never easy. Anybody who tries to tell you anything differently is a liar. It is indeed difficult especially if a person never develops any hobbies or skills of any sort. For those people, prison time can go by ever so slowly. It is almost as if time stands still, Some of what they show you in the movies about what goes on in prison is pretty much an accurate depiction but then again, they don't show you everything that really goes on. Believe me when I tell you that it's actually 100 times worse. You constantly have to be on guard watching everyone who comes within your proximity. You see everyone as a potential threat to your life until they have proven to you otherwise. My nature and personality made me likable to everyone but that was not always necessarily a good thing. Being a likable spirit will always pose a threat to somebody else. Jealousy, rivalries and people who were just mean spirited people were always at odds with me and everyone else. They found the most stupid reasons to instigate or agitate a situation. For example, if I interacted with certain persons or groups and another person had a beef with that person or group, then that automatically brought me into the conflict merely for association.

Just as it was in school where there existed cliques, the same thing existed in the prison system. Jocks hung with jocks, nerds hung with nerds, gays hung with gays and so on and so on. I tried to get along with everyone and that sometimes rubbed people the wrong way who were affiliated with these types of groups. It seemed that they made it their personal business to be concerned about my own personal business. This made it extremely difficult to cope with my situation which made it even more difficult to befriend or trust anybody.

I sorta found myself becoming more reclusive yet trying to keep my bubbly spirited nature in tact. Eventually I began to spend more time alone which made things even worse. Time started to go by slower and and slower and frustrations began to occupy the space that used to house my inner peace. I mean, you actually get to know every spot on the walls even down to the small details of the sizes of the paint bubbles on the wall. As time began to pass I started to realize that I had to do something to at least make it seem like time was moving faster because otherwise, I was starting to lose my damned mind up in there. I had a passion burning in me to want to help my fellow inmates cope with this unfortunate circumstance in life that we were all faced with but couldn't quite figure out how I could accomplish this without making enemies.

Now, it is very important that I mention the fact that my sister Janice was one of my biggest supporters while I was in prison serving my time. She had made a promise to me that she would never forsake me. She told me that she would always be there for me no matter what. There were so many times when she would visit me regardless of what kind of hardship it caused to her own financial situation. Many times when she didn't have a car, she would rent a car to come and see me. She would either bring mama or sometimes she would bring a female friend just so that I could have a companion who I could get to know and become pen pals with. One year I wanted Janice to come and visit me before the NFL Super Bowl. That particular day, it was a blizzard happening across the region. She told me that she wasn't going to be able to make it because her boyfriend didn't want her out on the road but I wanted a visit so bad and she came and saw me anyway and also brought me some money. She was one of the very reasons I was able to keep some sense of sanity. My brother Ralph was also one of my biggest supporters. Ralph would come often as possible to visit and bring money as well. He was a Police officer and so he couldn't always come but definitely made sacrifices just so I wouldn't be left in there alone to feel forsaken. With his connections in the Police Department, Ralph would later be a vital and instrumental player in my eventual release from prison which I will talk about later.

Chapter 6
Losing Tracy And
Gaining a Friendship for Life

I had been told by other people about a new prison facility being built up in the thumb area of Michigan in a city called Lapeer. Many of the inmates wanted to go there. Selection for it was based on a few things with the first factor being a first come, first served basis. Those who wanted to be transferred over to that unit had to put their name on a list. Other factors used in selecting who would go to that facility were that you basically had to either be on good behavior or had previously lived in that area at the time you caught your case initially and got sent to prison. I guess in retrospect, it was more or less a facility for the families of those who were incarcerated as a convenience to them so they could visit with less hardship on their finances thus eliminating long drives and travel expenses for most of them.

Being that it was a brand new facility, of course anybody in their right mind would jump at the opportunity to be in a brand spanking new clean environment especially since Ionia was one of the oldest facilities in Michigan but honestly, I wasn't really interested in going there at first. My lack of interest was mainly because I had become content with where I was mainly because I had enrolled in college studying law and was comfortable with my professors. I had also developed strong friendships with some of the men in there and really didn't want to leave that comfort zone I existed in.

I was happy to leave that dirty nasty place in Ionia though even though I felt I might not be able to get the same education. It was definitely a great uncertainty. When I got off the bus and looked at that prison, it looked like a college campus. All of those fears immediately washed away. We were the first inmates who were populated into that prison. It always feels good to be the first at something and in this case as compared to where I had just come from, it was definitely a good feeling to be among the first inmates to be at that new facility even though it was still and always will be a prison. We had the unique opportunity of breaking in the new correction officers. They didn't know what to expect from us so we kinda laid the foundation. Many times, they would ask us if they should write us up a or someone else for a misconduct or not. That is how much of a novice many of them were. Since it was a new facility, we were able to convince the administrators to have many programs and add performing arts and stuff like that into the system as a way to keep much of the in-house crime and hostilities at a minimum especially the gang related type of violence.

Now, LJ ended up coming to the Thumb Regional Correctional Facility in Lapeer as well. Even though I didn't show any feelings I harbored against LJ to him, our relationship became gloomy after we had gone to court. I think it was mostly because everybody kept asking him and me why did he get less time than me. People in the prison system already knew about our case because of the high media attention and many of the people in prison were from Flint. It was public knowledge whenever someone got sent back to court also so, every knew about everybody. LJ was only doing a15 year stint and I was doing 25 years-life. Some of the inmates would ask LJ "what did you do to get lesser time, did you snitch on somebody?" In those moments I knew our relationship would never be the same. LJ looked at me one day and asked me if I was going to get an appeal. I told him, they probably won't ever give me an appeal. He looked at me and lowered his head and walked away. I knew it was time to start forging new friendships and new alliances.

I ended up befriending a Muslim dude named Salih. This brother was so gifted. He had been in prison for 9 months and ended up being sent to Lapeer. He came into the system with a reputation already being that one of his brothers is a member of a famous group. I knew of his family and we all went to the same elementary school but in different grades. He and his family knew many of my cousins because they also went to school together and a few of them actually dated each other so indirectly, we already had a connection concerning family. One thing I can honestly say to this day is that Salih has always maintained that sense of integrity and I am certain that Islam has a lot to do with who he became and who he still is to this day. He became an image of his father who I hold with such high regard and respect. His father was the resident Imam at one of the Masjids locally. Every other Friday, he would come up to the Thumb Regional Correctional Facility and teach the Friday Jumah Prayer service. We all called him Imam Wali.

Imam Wali was a dynamic speaker but his strong point in his teaching style was that he acted more like a father figure to the prisoners rather than just a member of the clergy. He had a lot of influence in the Flint community and it carried with him to the prison as he mentored us with such great wisdom and patience. Plus because his son was in Prison, this allowed for him an opportunity to see his son more often. Do you see how mysteriously God works? You see, his son was also in prison for a crime he didn't commit. With his father being an Imam, this allowed him to see his father more often which in turn benefited me.

I got to spend time away from my cell and I had the honor of learning a new religion and at the same time, formed a strong bond with Salih and his father. I eventually accepted Islam and became a Muslim. I started attending the Jumah Prayer services on a regular consistent basis. Imam Wali told me to keep my faith and trust in Allah. He told me that it was so hard coming to the prison to teach and then have to leave that facility without his son. He told me to take advantage of every opportunity given to me to do good deeds for my spirit. Salih would always reach out to me and make sure I was attending Jumah. As we would end our night on Thursday nights, he was always sure to say, "I'll see you at Jumah tomorrow."

81

Speaking of Jumah, I remember one time when we were about to have Jumah prayer service and I was asked to call the Athan which is the prayer call which alerts the believers that it is time for prayer. Now, keep in mind that I am a big dude. At that time, I looked almost as big as body builder Arnold Schwarzenegger. Ok well, maybe not Schwarzenegger but close to it, ha ha ha. Anyway, I always had a huge muscular frame and so what came out of my mouth was totally unexpected. I stood up and looked around the room at everyone and with a strong confidence in my singing ability I opened my mouth and began to make the prayer call. Everyone struggled to suppress their laughter as they had to sit there and listen to me. Instead of chanting the call with a strong deep masculine voice, I have no earthly idea why I chanted that call in a high soprano tone. It was hilarious to everyone in the room. And the funniest part about it was that I kept going. The laughter didn't stop me from handling my business. They all were sitting their laughing to the point their intestines were about to burst and yet I tuned them out and continued to chant in my high pitched soprano. When I was finished, I politely went and sat down with everyone else while thinking in my mind with great confidence, "go on with your bad self."

After Jumah was over, Salih was cracking up at me and couldn't stop laughing. His laughter even caused me to laugh even harder than him. It was one of the funniest moments I had in that prison and Salih and I reflect back on that day often. That's what made our friendship so special. We could laugh at each other without thinking about being upset and we always had each others backs. We could critique each other and never take offense even though I was the one mostly being critiqued. The bond I formed with him felt as if we were even more close than blood brothers. Every day before we went back to our respective cells for permanent lock-down for the rest of the night, we made sure to say to each other, I love you bro and we didn't care if anybody interpreted that as being involved with some gay shit. Besides, everyone knew Salih was strict in his religious beliefs and practices and therefore had no doubt that he was definitely not gay and they knew I loved women and so they just had to respect the brotherly love for what it was. Even though he was all about his religion, I always loved how he kept his sense of humor.

One day I was eating some fried chicken. It was an 8 piece box of chicken made by Banquet. Salih asked me could he get some of the chicken and I told him yes he could have some. He was expecting me to let him grab some right from the box that I as eating from but instead, I told him that I would be back in a few minutes. I went and purchased him a box of his own because I knew I wanted all of mine for myself and planned to eat every single piece in that box. We laughed so hard about that. He thought it was so comical of me to go and buy him his own box instead of just sharing a couple of pieces with him. What he didn't understand about me is that I could eat 2 boxes of that chicken by myself.

If I had given him some then I would have had to buy some more anyway. That's just how big my appetite was. Salih and I both always tried to have each others back. If someone tried to be aggressive toward him, I was ready and willing to defend this brother with my life. He was the same way toward me. If someone spoke out of line toward me, that brother was ready to jump in and take somebody down if need be. He spent a lot of time in the gym like me. He didn't go there trying to bulk up with muscle like me. Instead, he went there for strength and training. He was very skilled in boxing having learned by watching Muhammad Ali when he was younger and from sparring with one of his brothers.

That Salih was so quick with his hands and for a small framed man, he possessed a lot of power in his punches. One time, he was working with the punching bag. He didn't realize it but he was punching so swiftly and his punches were so hard that almost the entire yard stopped and started watching him. I understand now what I didn't understand back then. He was putting everyone on notice. He was letting them all know that if they ever tried to come at him the wrong way, they were going to be in for a battle for their life. I was and remain ever so grateful he and I became such good friends. It's not that I needed any protection or nothing like that but people knew Salih and I were friends and hung together all the time. They knew that a fight with me meant a fight with Salih and by virtue of that display he put on with that punching bag, I was certain no body wanted a piece of me or him. In the world we lived in, you needed allies and I couldn't imagine having a more greater person in my corner other than my brother Salih.

About a month after meeting Salih, I joined this group called the Jaycees which is a group that helps charities such as the Salvation Army. They often allow prisoners to have small chapter affiliation groups. Part of what they let us do is have fundraisers. These types of endeavors required the approval of the warden and to my surprise we did get that approval. Working with them allowed for us to have restaurant pizza and you can't imagine how good it felt to eat some real pizza after being locked up so long without that little simple pleasure. We also had donuts. Eating those donuts and pizza made us feel like we had just hit the jackpot in the lottery.

Jaycees had set a 17,000 dollar target for our fundraiser endeavor and I was the chairman of that charter. I called the fund raiser, KIDS AT RISK. After we had successfully finished with our fundraiser, they held a banquet at the prison in our honor and two members of our family were allowed to come to the banquet. I was so excited to the point that I had to ask them again for re-assurance. Do you mean that we actually get to invite 2 of our family members for real? Immediately, I told them, I'm going to invite my mother and my sister Janice. At the banquet we were allowed to sit at the dinner table with our family inside the prison at the gymnasium. That was a priceless moment.

My mom sat there next to me as one of the guards said to her, "Mr. Moore is a good man, he don't give us any problems and we didn't think he could pull this off but he raised 17,000 dollars to give to the Ionia chapter of the make a wish foundation this year". I must have smiled from ear to ear hearing him say those things to my mama knowing that while in prison I was able to help 60 needy kids. They let us take pictures and it was such an exhilarating experience. I got to wear a suit and tie and I finally had a chance to eat like a normal person. They had napkins and silverware on our table like they have in restaurants with place cards with our name on them along with our family. I went up to the buffet looking for a spork to use because we weren't allowed to use forks in prison because of the danger they posed. They could be used as a weapon. When I got back to the table I noticed that my mother and sister had unrolled their napkins exposing their silverware. I saw their knives and forks and asked with inquisitive excitement, how did you all get that?

I'm holding the sporks in my hand as I asked them this question. They looked around at all of the other tables and said to me, "everybody has them. See, you have one too." Then I unraveled my napkin and said look, its a fork, I got me a fork and its shiny. I was holding it up in the air as if it were diamond or crystal. I clanked it against my teeth in excitement. They just looked at me smiling in admiration at the joyful moment I was experiencing that people who are free take for granted. For dinner, we had Turkey and dressing and cranberry sauce. It was basically like a Thanksgiving menu with pies and everything. Mama was looking at me as if I were a little kid opening Christmas presents or something and wore her ever so humble smile as I was overcome with excitement. I was sure to use that knife to cut my turkey trying to show off my cutting skills..

I stuffed my napkin in my shirt as if I were in a real restaurant. It felt so good. I really can't put into words how something as simple as that brought so much joy for that brief moment. It made me feel in that brief time that I was on the outside even though I was still confined on the inside. My sister Janice put me on blast though and brought a little humor to the table when she asked, "why you so excited about using silverware when you used to eat with your hands?" Everyone who heard burst out laughing. After the banquet was over, we took more pictures and then hugged each other as we bid farewell. I still cherish that day and I always will.

Salih and I continued trying to help make prison life somewhat tolerable even though being in prison is a living hell and an everlasting nightmare to say the least. We held banquets every year after fasting the month of Ramadan. This wasn't the case before Salih came to the prison however. Before he arrived, Muslims were barely allowed to practice their religion. When Salih arrived at that facility, he and his father helped to change all of that. They were the reason the prison system changed their policies to allow Muslims our right to observe our religion which meant celebrating the ending of Ramadan for 3 days which is called Eid. Through his brother Clark, he contracted with outside caterers who brought food from outside the prison in for us to eat during the Eid celebrations. Those type of experiences are what I still treasure to this day. It is mainly because those experiences connected me with the outside world in a sense. Food from outside the prison was always considered a privileged delicacy and any time away from our cells was always a blessing. I needed those times away and looked forward to Ramadan every year.

I also looked forward to those expected and unexpected visits from mama, Janice and my brother Ralph too. Janice kept her promise and visited me often and tried her best to help me to know and believe I was not in this alone. Ralph made sure I had whatever I needed. Mama, I mean what can I say about this beautiful woman to help you all understand what she means to me. There are really no words that appropriately describe how I feel about her. Without her, Janice, Salih and Ralph in my life, I would have struggled harder to keep my sanity in an insane prison environment sharing space with insane people. Ralph is one of the very reasons I am free to this day which I will explain later. I am forever indebted to him for what he sacrificed for me in giving me his time, financial help, legal expertise and all of those wonderful visits. Those visits from him, mama, my sister, the rest of my family and all of my friends were so important to me. Even if it were only 5 minutes away from that cell, I was grateful because I made those 5 minutes feel like 5 hours. I would even get called out on visits by Salih's family and friends.

He would have one of his family members call me out on a visit when they came to visit him just so I could get out of my cell for however long or brief. You all can never understand how valuable those visits were and how they helped me and Salih keep our sanity in a place where insanity was normal for most. Those times out of that cell were precious and cherished moments and I will always be grateful for everyone who came to visit especially my brother Ralph, my sister Janice and mama who as I have stated was my rock. Both of them were my rocks but mama was the rock and the glue. Mama couldn't always come up for visits because she worked at a factory and so her job occupied most of her time which was certainly understandable. Mama was always the type of person who did what she had to do. She was one of my main sources of financial support during that whole time I was in that awful experience. Soon, however, visits became far and few and I had to accept the fact that my family and friends had to earn their respective livings and so I couldn't expect to see them every week.

Then that unfortunate day came when they rode Salih out of the prison we were in and took him to another facility without any advance notice. Privately I cried like a baby because they took my best friend away and I was fearing I would probably never see him again. I tried to find out where they were sending him so I could keep in touch but none of the administration members would tell me. I felt that they were deliberately trying to keep us away from each other. You see, Salih was directly responsible for getting music and performing arts into the prison as a way to allow the prisoners to channel their frustrations and energies into something positive. He helped change the prison experience into something that was more manageable for prisoners which in turn was a big help to the DOC. This caused great concern for me because although I knew he could take care of himself, I needed to know he was ok. We had each others back where we were and now I wasn't there to look out for him the way he looked out for me.

Months went by without knowing where my brother had went. Finally I did hear from him and wondered what the heck took him so long to contact me. He told me that he had written me several times. I later found out that the prison had been keeping the letters for whatever reason. By law, they were supposed to release any letter addressed to an inmate within 24 hours but they kept them and gave them to us when they felt like it. I became angry at the system for doing that to me and my friend. He was more than just a friend or protector. He was a teacher to me and all of the other inmates. He would always admonish us when we acted wrongfully and reminded us of the proper conduct we should always strive to follow. I became a Muslim because of him teaching me the religion and for that I owe him a great debt of gratitude. He saved my life by introducing Islam to me and they had the nerve and audacity to conceal letters this magnificent brother was sending me. I was more than ready to take on the establishment and higher ups in power and began filing grievances against them for any infractions they committed against me. I was not going to let them get away with nothing else after that.

It finally had dawned on me exactly what they were doing. You see, many prisoners like myself and Salih were innocent and wrongfully convicted and didn't belong in prison. We weren't getting into fights or receiving any type of disciplinary actions or tickets counted against us. They didn't like that. They wanted us to act a fool and get disciplined so that when it was time to go before parole, we would easily be denied parole due to conduct infractions against us. When they can't goat us into doing things to get us in trouble, they ride us out and send us to a different prison. This causes a person to have to start all over again making friendships, alliances and gaining trust among fellow inmates. The chances of getting into trouble increases each time a person is sent to another facility. They didn't want prisoners accepting Islam either and thus becoming devout servants like Salih who treated people the way Allah orders us to treat them. They wanted monsters and predators up in there. As long as they could keep monsters and predators in there, they could keep extending their time in prison. This meant job security for them so they needed Salih gone.

I was determined to prove to them that it didn't matter where they sent me, I wasn't going to change who I am and how I respond to situations. I always believed that someday I would walk out of there a free man and I was equally confident that Salih would do the same. I knew someday we would have the last laugh because even if we never saw each other ever again, we became brothers in spirit and that is something they could never take away from us or separate us from. We believe in the oneness of God and so that makes us companions in the hereafter regardless of what happens in this physical life. Even so, I was still determined to get the last laugh in this life which eventually happened. I will elaborate on that later.

Soon after Salih had been shipped out, Ralph stopped coming as often because of his job and mama and Janice weren't coming up as often either. Tracy would still try to come as often as she could but even her visits began to become too far and few in between occurrences. Janice would bring Tracy up to the prison to visit me all the time. Those visits were always special to me because Tracy was my heart. She stood by me that whole time throughout the time after my arrest and after I was sent to prison and never wavered in her love and support. She believed in me. She would always tell me that no matter what, she was going to stick by me. During the visits when I was in the county jail, we had to speak through a glass window but once I got to prison things were much better. We got to sit next to each other and hold hands and hug and kiss each other and it felt awesome to have those moments with her. She had a daughter who I treated as though she was my own daughter. She would bring her up to the prison with her sometimes so that I could see her.

I can't really begin to explain what those visits meant to me. We spent even more time together when I got transferred to the facility in Lapeer, Michigan because Lapeer was only about 15 miles from Flint. This lasted for a few years. Then I got transferred back to the Michigan Reformatory in Ionia which was about an hour and a half away from Flint. She still came to visit as she had done when I had been in Ionia when I was first sent to prison but not as often as she was able to come when I was in Lapeer

Then sadly, one week, I didn't hear from her. I tried to get my sister to contact her but she wasn't answering her phone. I started getting angry at her because she knew how much those visits meant to me because it allowed me to get out of that prison cell for about an hour every time she came up. Then one day I got called up to the counselors office for a phone call. When you get called up to the counselors office, its usually because the call is very important and they don't want you in population with the other inmates because the call may be bad news and usually about a family member or close friend. While I was being led to that office, my heart began racing because I knew something was wrong because otherwise they wouldn't be taking me there. Those type of calls are always emergency calls and so I kept trying to figure out who could it be that was calling me and for what purpose. It was January 5th. When I answered the phone, it was my mother on the phone. A huge sigh of relief temporarily came over me because hearing her voice assured me that mama was ok.

She said, "I've got some sad news to tell you, they found Tracy." I paused and then I said, huh? She repeated, saying, "they found Tracy." So I'm thinking oh ok, finally somebody knows where she's at. I asked mama where had she been all that time and why hadn't been up to the prison to see me. Then mama gave me the most devastating news which no person ever wants to hear. She said, "I'm so sorry to have to tell you this. Tracy is dead." She told me that they found Tracy dead in the garage still sitting in her car. She had been poisoned by carbon monoxide. She had fallen asleep in the car while waiting for it to warm up with the car still running. She had been dead for almost a whole week. Riga mortise had begun to set in and her skin as I had been told had turned a few shades darker. I bowed my head down and burst out in tears spewing out uncontrolled emotions. I was devastated. Tracy stood by me in my worst hour of life and now she was gone forever. There I was stuck in a prison feeling powerless and devastated.

I couldn't grasp a hold of why she of all people had to be taken from me. My baby was gone and I didn't know how I was going to get through all of this without her. It was extremely hard trying to interact with everyone else while trying to conceal what I was going through. I wanted to go to her funeral but because we were only boyfriend and girlfriend and not married, the administrators in the prison wouldn't let me go pay my respects and say goodbye to the love of my life. It hurt so bad not to be able to say goodbye to her and although I was devastated, I tried to keep my composure and not become angry because I couldn't go pay my respects. I had to suck that pain up. Sadly, after her death however, I lost contact with my daughter who I held dear to my heart. I turned to God to help me through it all. I questioned Him about why this had to happen. I needed some answers.

Tracy was the other half of me. She was my heart and soul and even though she was so young, she was mature enough to know what she wanted in life and I am so grateful I had the pleasure and honor of spending time on this earth with her. I don't care what a government document says or doesn't say. Tracy was my wife and I was her husband. That's how we lived our lives. We were together as one. She was my ride or die and I'll always love her with all my heart. I just needed to understand why she was taken from this earth so young. During that devastating period, I ached so much in my heart. I asked the Warden if I could be transferred back to Lapeer Michigan so that I could be closer to my daughter to which he obliged. I needed to see her and help her get through this. She also became my own therapy because seeing her again brought so much joy and fulfillment into my spirit. I believe that became the turning point in my life that drew me closer to God and helped me to fully define what I wanted and needed to do with my life.

A few months passed. I called mama to see how she was doing and she told me that my friend Robin had made contact with her and wanted to come up to the prison to see me. She came up to see me one day. I had met Robin before I had went to prison. As I stated earlier, my sister Sherry was in

92

New Paths halfway house. She was allowed to leave the facility on weekends to visit with family. One day after she had been visiting over the weekend, I drove her back to New Paths. As I was dropping her off, I noticed Robin and spoke to her. I let her know that I was interested in her. Initially she had rejected me citing that I was too young for her and that it was against policy to have any kind of relationship with friends or family members of inmates. I kept persistently trying to get with her whenever I took Sherry back to New Paths and eventually she gave in. Tracy and I had known each other since childhood and had this love and hate relationship. We would break up for a few months and then get back together. I met Robin during one of those periods when Tracy and I had broken up.

Me and Robin didn't really have a relationship in the sense of the way a boyfriend and girlfriend act in a relationship because she remained firm in her decision to uphold the policy because she needed her job. We were intimate on occasions however, but never really considered ourselves in a real relationship. Since we didn't really have a defined relationship, this made it much easier for me and Tracy to get back together. Tracy remained my permanent woman until the day she passed away. When Robin came to visit, she was definitely a welcomed sight because I needed some kind of diversion to take my mind off of the loss of Tracy because I felt that a part of me died with Tracy. I didn't just jump right into a relationship with her. I was still grieving over the loss of Tracy and Robin understood the boundaries. She knew that although I was not afraid to love again, I certainly was not looking for it and needed to heal. During that first visit, she told me some news I was not expecting to hear.

She told me she had a 5 year old daughter. Her next words sent me into total shock and numbness momentarily when she then informed me I was the father. I couldn't believe what I was hearing coming from her mouth. Are you serious?

I have a 5 year old daughter and I am just now finding out about it. Naturally I asked if she was sure I was the father. She told me that she was certain and that she was not with anyone else beside me during that time. Now keep in mind that she was strict about not being in a relationship because of the job policy so it made sense that I was most likely the father. She suggested a DNA test. She told me that her, I mean our daughter was eager to meet me and asked if it was ok to bring her up for a visit to which I obliged.

When she came back with our daughter, all it took was one look at that beautiful little princess and my heart melted. I looked at her and right then and there I knew there was absolutely no need to take a DNA test. She had many of my features and I knew she was mine. The very first words she said to me as she gave me the warmest hug were; "this my daddy." I was so humbled and proud in that moment and wished it could last forever. I had me a beautiful daughter. Now I had two beautiful little princesses who were giving me even more incentive to gain my freedom. I needed to be in their lives and I didn't want to do that from behind prison walls. I kept contact with her and now that I am free, I see her all the time and I love her with all my heart. Robin would come as often as she could and our relationship began to grow. We decided to get married. We were allowed to have a wedding ceremony at the prison. Imam Wali who at that time was still the resident Imam at Flint, Masjid came to the prison and he was the one who married us.

Robin became my new rock. She became one of my biggest supporters. She would visit me at every facility regardless of how far away they sent me. She would drive 8 hours all the way up to Marquette to visit and even through blizzard conditions if need be. She sent me money all the time to help me and kept me supplied with the necessities of life and with money to support my eating habits. Robin began to notice the same women coming up for visits. Outside of the prison, people didn't understand why a woman would have a relationship with a man serving a long prison sentence. After noticing the same women all of the time, Robin began making friendships with these women. To help people understand how life is for the wives and girlfriends of prisoners, she decided to write an article explaining this from their vantage point. This article was initially published in a news paper from the Thumb region but was later published in the Flint Journal as well. She continued tying to be a champion in the cause of misunderstood women who had relationships with men serving time. We stayed together for 12 years.

Then one day, the unthinkable happened. I caught a bogus charge and as a consequence, she apparently believed the accusations laid against me and broke up with me and filed for divorce. I will explain more about that incident later. Before that incident however, I must say that I had a great relationship with Robin. She taught me a lot about responsibility and how a woman wants and deserves to be treated. I can honestly say I have learned so much from her and my only regret is that I didn't learn it soon enough because I cared deeply for her and I know she cared deeply for me.

There was a dry spell when visits were becoming hard to come by. People had their own lives to live and I understood that. Ralph was a police officer, mama worked at the factory and everyone else had jobs and families to tend to. Weeks began to turn into months without visits. As time lingered on, I needed to occupy my time during those dry periods when family and friends weren't able to come up to visit me. I started going to the weight room lifting weights. I was already a big dude and once I started lifting weights my big physique began to swell up into a well defined muscular specimen. They all called me Big Moe up in there because I was so massive in size. In addition to weight training and exercise, I enrolled back into college to occupy my time. I became highly interested in the law after seeing so many law books in the library.

I started reading so many law cases trying to figure out what I could do to undo my predicament and get myself out of prison expeditiously. The more I studied, the more I learned and the more I learned, the more passionate I became about law. I had rapidly started developing a more in depth understanding what our rights were and yes, this includes the rights of prisoners too. I studied and studied trying to understand every aspect of the law hoping to find any and all legal remedies to help myself and my fellow inmates. This became the one thing which converted former enemies into friends. I had developed a reputation for being very knowledgeable concerning law to the point that everyone would come to me for help with their cases. I was now able to serve my time in prison with a new found purpose. I needed this as much as they needed me.

The more I learned about the law, the more I burned with passion wanting to do more with that knowledge to help bring true justice to our prison society and society as a whole to prevent young men and women from ending up in situations which lead them to prison. I eventually graduated and earned my degree and became a para legal. Soon, everyone began to swarm all over me wanting me to help them with their cases. Word of mouth began to increase my popularity. This happened all because I had started developing an impeccable record of successes in helping inmates fight grievances against the prison system and in many cases helping some inmates get out of prison altogether. It rose to the point that I had to start charging for my time as a little side hustle to earn money for my personal needs. Hey, I had to do what I had to do up in there and every penny counts so if it meant having a side hustle then I was game for whatever.

Everybody started looking to me "Big Moe" to help them out with their cases. In addition to this turning out to be a lucrative business venture, it brought to me something I never imagined that prison life could possibly bring. It brought me a sense of true purpose. I found myself being needed in a high demand fashion and that caused me to want to feel the need to be there as crazy as that may sound. I was needed in there because I was highly efficient at what I did for those inmates.

Case after case was being won by inmates because of the help I had given them and naturally, that boosted my desire even higher. I was on a roll. It was the perfect tradeoff. I got to do something good to help somebody, got paid for it and more importantly, they were getting justice for themselves that they weren't getting before and as for me, it made my time in there go much faster. When you are passionate at something you are doing, time always seems to move faster and that was indeed the case for me.

As I saw how much I was making a difference in the lives of these men, I knew than that someday I wanted to use this knowledge and experience to become a motivational speaker helping people on the outside. I kept maintaining my belief that prison was not my home and someday I would be a free man and I would dedicate my life to being a mentor to people who were lost or susceptible to hanging out with the wrong crowd. I was determined that someday I would make a difference. Many of the young people I know I'll probably end up trying to mentor will be without fathers and sometimes their mothers as well. I hope to be an inspiration to them so they won't waste time not having relationships with their parents. Prison caused me to lose so much time with mama and daddy. Both of them tried to stay in my life and visit as often as possible. I spent more time with mama than daddy though. My dad made effort to see me and to me that's worth 1 million visits.

Make no mistake, dad had come up to visit many times and I enjoyed seeing him. I just wish he could have made it up there more often than he did but I understood his circumstances. Sometimes mama would even bring him up to see me when he didn't have a car. The first thing he would always do when he saw me was give me a big hug. When we embraced, it was always a long and warm embrace as if neither of us wanted to ever let go of one another. We would talk about everything. He was so laid back even though I knew inside he was struggling with my incarceration and felt so helpless because he couldn't get me out of there. One time, I called daddy and we talked on the phone for a while. As the conversation was nearing it's end, we were talking about me walking out of those prison doors someday. Daddy said, "son, I know you're going to be free one day. I just don't know if I'll be alive to see that day when it happens." I said, daddy don't talk like that. He said, "I don't know son, I just haven't been feeling myself lately. I just don't know." I said well don't talk like that because I'm getting out of here. He said, "I love you son. I said love you too pop."

Then one day one of the correction officers called me out of my cell. I was sent to that special room where they put you in quarantine whenever you receive bad news. I wasn't prepared for no bad news. They had told me that I needed to call mama. I called her. First she asked me how was I doing, and I told her I was okay. Then I asked, whats wrong mama, why did they want me to call you? She said, they found your father dead. I yelled out the words, WHAT! She then said he's gone baby, I'm so sorry. I had learned even before I went to prison how to deal with death and I always tried to be strong whenever a loved one passed away. I always believed that since we want a better life beyond this life, we should rejoice rather than mourn, but that was my pops. I burst into tears. I told mama, I wanted to go to the funeral. After I hung up from mama, I sat there in disbelief. My pops was gone.

The guards gave me a few moments to collect myself before taking me back to my cell. As they escorted me to my cell, I couldn't stop thinking about my father. My tears began flowing again. I didn't care about no man code and how men are not supposed to cry. That was my father. As I continued to cry, I said aloud, I'm going to miss you pop, I'm going to miss you man. I started to get dizzy and then I collapsed. The guards tried to catch me. They helped me to my cell and I just stayed in solitude in overwhelming sorrow and disbelief. My pops was gone. They asked me did I want to go the funeral and I said yes. They told me it would cost $1500 to pay for them to send armed guards with me to the funeral. I immediately got on the phone and made a few calls and gathered up enough money to cover the costs. My sister Sherry was still in prison at the time as well and she was able to get enough money to go say goodbye to daddy.

On the day of the funeral, they informed me that I hadn't got the money to them in time and so they weren't letting me go to the funeral. I was highly pissed. I was certain I had met the deadline. I got the money to them within a day and a half before the deadline. My heart was already broken and now it was being crushed because I couldn't go home and say goodbye to my pops. It was treatment like that which continued to be the fuel I needed to give that extra thrust pushing me forward in my efforts to get home for good. I started back focusing more on studying law again. I had actually begun to miss that high passion I used to have when I was in college studying law.

You see, back then while I was in college, I had written an essay detailing how the prison industry had been turning the prison system into a lucrative business. In this essay, I showed how the prison system had become a revolving door and thus basically recycling many of the same prisoners right back into the prison. Some viewed my actions as heroic and yet others saw me as being a snitch. I receive a visit from a professor from the University of Michigan who came to ask my permission for her to publish my essay in an article she was writing. I of course said yes to her because I felt that any opportunity to have my voice heard translated into hope. That particular article somehow reached some very powerful people in government. It somehow got the attention of Michigan Senator Carl Levin.

He came up to the prison and directly spoke to me about the article and the concerns I and the prisoners were having. He gave me permission to continue to keep in touch by writing him because he took my complaints and concerns very seriously. You should have seen the faces of all of the officials within that prison. Their faces seemed to carry a sense of worry and uncertainty wondering what a high ranking Senator within the United states government was doing sitting across from me in a private meeting. From the warden all the way down to the newest officers, everyone was seemingly shaking in their boots. Even the prisoners were watching and wondering. This was not necessarily a good thing however as I stated before and it would prove to be a big reason why I am here today telling you my story. You see, some had indeed interpreted that visit as me being another snitch who needed to be dealt with.

Still however, in spite of the potential threat I posed to those who took issue with my actions, I remained vigilant. I wrote letters to any and everybody who I thought had some kind of power or influence that would listen to me. I sent letters to Quincy Jones, Oprah Winfrey, congressmen and congresswomen and many others. I never received any letters back from Quincy or Oprah but I still kept hope and belief that someday I would go home a free man. Years later, I had learned about another powerful man like Nelson Mandela who we all know had been a political activist and had spent 27 years in prison as a political enemy. His name was Geronimo Pratt. He was the Godfather of rapper Tupac Shakur. He had spent 27 years in prison just like Mandela. Famous attorney Johnny Cochran had been his attorney when he had been sent to prison in 1969. Johnny Cochran had vowed to get him out someday. I had heard about Johnny Cochran during the OJ Simpson trial and wanted to reach out to him hoping that he could help me get out of prison too. I don't know if OJ Simpson was guilty or not and so I post no judgment for or against him but when Johnny Cochran go him an acquittal for a double murder charge, I knew then I needed him to help me so I reached out to him.

I had written a brief which contained a motion that I was seeking on behalf of a person I had been giving legal advice to. I sent it to the Cooley Law College and somehow it ended up in the hands of Johnny Cochran and his law firm. I received a letter from one of the para legals within his law firm asking me to write a brief for them. I felt so honored firstly that they had even read and appreciated my work and secondly that they thought so highly of my work that they wanted me to write one for them. Of course, this caused my passion to grow even stronger. They used that motion in one of their cases and that motion was filed in the United States Supreme Court.

That event made history because although many inmates had written their own motions and briefs, I was the first prisoner in United States history to file a motion that was heard in the Supreme Court. I felt so passionate to the point that I started writing out grievances against the Prisons and DOC for everything that we felt were injustices. Whether it was a grievance to get hot meals into the prison or to get blankets into the prison during the winter, I was willing and ready to take their butts to court. Even though they seemed like trivial things to people in the outside world, they were huge to us in prison. They were denying us some of the basic common sense things every human being should have in life. Their actions rose to the level of cruel and unusual punishment in our minds and though we were prisoners, we never gave up our right to be equally protected under the law.

I wrote to Johnny Cochran to explain what happened in my case hoping to solicit his help. I received a visit from him. Yes, you read that right. Johnny Cochran came to visit me directly in the prison. It was one of my most treasured and memorable moments in my life. I kept the visitor pass which had his name on it. All of my family and fellow inmates were so proud for me in that moment because they knew the magnitude of that day and what it possibly meant to me and my freedom. After our visit, he assured me that from that point moving forward, we became friends.

He said that he would use every ounce of his wisdom, legal expertise and resources to help set me free. He told me personally that he had vowed all of those years to get Geronimo Pratt out of prison because that loss he suffered in court was a devastating loss to him and he needed to right that wrong. He told me not to give up the fight because he didn't give up the fight for Geronimo Pratt. You see, Geronimo Pratt was on death row for all those years for a crime he didn't commit and this bothered Johnny Cochran throughout his life. He told me that in 1992 he had exhausted all of the remedies he had and the Supreme Court had shot him down each time. Basically as a result of this, Mr Pratt was going to be executed and was awaiting the day when they would come to announce when his sentence would be carried out. Then in 1997, Johnny said he threw one last ditch Hail Mary effort and was able to get him out.

Mandela had spent 27 years and walked out of those prison doors a free man and now Geronimo Pratt who spent 27 years on death row walked out of those prison doors a free man. He told me that I too will walk away someday so I must never ever give up hope. With that new sense of hope, I set out to study law even more in depth to find anything in legal case history which I could use to hopefully someday help set myself free. I didn't just want to place my fate in his hands although he was a very capable attorney who had a proven track record. It was my life and I needed to have a say in my fate and I was never going to accept prison as my home. It was a daunting task but I was very much motivated and ready to do whatever I needed to do because I wanted my freedom. I started contacting every organization I could think of. From the American Civil Liberties Union to the NAACP, I contacted everyone. I even sent letters to them on behalf of my fellow inmates continuing in my efforts to bring justice to the prisoners for the mistreatment and denial of such basic common sense human needs.

This didn't really set well with the prison system though because I was exposing them. It forced them to give some concessions though because they didn't want to appear bad in public eye because of what I had been exposing even though unbeknownst to me, I had slowly been becoming a thorn in their side and was slowly and eventually becoming their enemy.

To us they weren't the DOC. We called them The Department of Corruption. Most of those prisons were privatized as privately owned businesses and each inmate represented money to the owners. With the Crime Bill passed by former President Bill Clinton and endorsed by his wife Hillary, private prisons began to be built all across the United States. They owned stock in the company which builds these private prisons so you can see why they wanted that bill passed. When I first went to prison just to give you an understanding of the magnitude of what I am saying to you, Michigan only had 11 prisons. Under Governor Engler who was Governor of Michigan during the Clinton administration and during the administrations which followed, Michigan prisons swelled from 11 to 52. To them, I believe incarceration was never about taking criminals off the streets. It was about making a profit off of crime.

During all of that time while the prisons were growing in numbers, I had been watching the news and keeping abreast of current events. I had come to realize that the powers that be were deliberately doing things politically and socially to ensure that many inner city minorities among both young men and young women would end up in these money making slave plantations called prisons. I began writing articles outlining these facts. I had started getting pubic notoriety for what I had been exposing as well as in the prison system.

Politicians and entertainers would come to visit me and so my popularity increased immensely. I felt I was on a roll. The more noise I made, the stronger my passion began to grow. I owe all of that inspiration to Allah first and foremost of course but also to Nelson Mandela and Geronimo Pratt for being the forces fueling my burning desire to make a difference. I know I can never say I deserve to be mentioned in the same sentence with them as great men championing the cause of justice but one thing I can say is that I strive hard to be just like them and carry that spirit of justice onward which they too carried.

One day Muhammad Ali and his wife visited the prison. Muhammad came there to speak to the prisoners offering us hope that someday we can become better human beings and do great things like him. Everyone of us including the prisoners and staff at the facility stood in awe because we were sharing the same space with the Greatest boxer of all times. We were all star struck and well deserving I might add. Ali is truly not only one of the greatest sports legends of all time but one of the greatest champions of justice our modern civilizations have ever seen. I had the pleasure and honor of talking to him and Lonnie Ali. I told both of them about my case and assured them I was innocent and was trying everything within my power to gain my freedom. Muhammad told me that he understood and had empathy for me and what I was going through.

He said that he visited boxer Iron Mike Tyson while he was in prison and that experience helped him understand the magnitude of what prisoners go through. Lonnie told me that both her and Muhammad Ali would keep me in their prayers and she gave me permission to keep in touch. It hurt me immensely when Muhammad Ali passed away because although I thanked him for listening and caring, I didn't get to have the pleasure of letting him know I am now a free man. Someday God willing, I plan to reach out to Lonnie because I am grateful for hers and Muhammad's influence in my life.

Throughout the years after Geronimo Pratt had been released, I continued to do as best to be a champion and advocate for justice in the prison for my fellow inmates. As I have alluded to this before, my actions created enemies within the prison system and in particular among the administration and powers that be behind the scenes. By this I mean, the private prison owners, their stock holders, political figures and investors who keep them in power. This became manifest to me when I was falsely accused of a crime. Keep in mind that I am 6'2 and at that time I weighed nearly 300 pounds of solid muscle. Now, it is extremely important that you understand something about the prison experience. It is a well known belief among prisoners that the easiest way to cause a prisoner to have more time added onto their sentence is to accuse them of rape or attempted murder against another inmate. The most targeted people who were always finding themselves being falsely accused were the biggest black men among the population.

I have been to prisons where the total population was over 1200 inmates and there were only approximately only about 30 to 40 white inmates in that whole facility so as a big muscular black man, I was an easy target for intimidation. They needed me silenced because I was exposing them. It is my firm belief that they wanted me silenced from the beginning. Once again for a second time in my life, I found myself being falsely accused of a crime I didn't commit and I was placed into maximum security after I had worked my way all the way down to minimum security which allowed for me to be among the trusted inmates.

They placed me into solitary confinement. While there, I had begun to get sick all the time and was being denied essential medical attention. I didn't think they were trying to kill me at first, but rather, I just believed they were being unjust to me in retaliation for my speaking out against them and for contacting pubic officials seeking outside help to get justice for me and my fellow inmates. Eventually I became so ill that they were forced to take me to the hospital. It was determined that I had been poisoned by arsenic. Now pause and ask yourself, how in the world is it even remotely possible for a prisoner to get his or her hands on some arsenic? You would have to come to the same conclusion which I came to which is that somebody from the outside made that possible and it had to come from someone who was very powerful to be able to number 1, get their hands on it and number 2, slip it in without being detected. They don't sell arsenic at the local pharmacy. It is a poisonous chemical so obviously someone with some powerful connections got their hands on it.

From that moment on, I knew someone wanted me dead. Now because arsenic was involved, and because of the false charges levied against me, the state Police were called to investigate. A female detective within the state police department came to do the interview. This interview took place on the same day of President Obama's Inauguration as the nation's first black president. During the interview, she asked me what did I think about President Obama becoming president and I told her I didn't want to talk about Obama. I told her I wanted to talk about what had just happened to me and that I wanted to know why I was being falsely accused of a crime and then all of a sudden I am being poisoned with arsenic. You see, I believed they were trying to kill me. By law they were supposed to investigate my claim and offer me protection even if I didn't ask for it. They have to offer it regardless. That is the law.

Keep in mind that she was from the state police which meant that she worked for the same entity I had a grievance against so there was an automatic conflict of interest and it showed in how she chose to deal with my complaint which was absolutely nothing. She ruled that she did not see enough evidence to prove there was a conspiracy to kill me even though I had documented proof from the hospital that I had been poisoned by arsenic. Who brought arsenic into the prison and who put it in my food? I needed those questions answered and yet she determined that there was not enough evidence in my case to investigate any further. What a joke. She was making a mockery of my intelligence and of the system of justice.

Now I need you to understand a few critical facts about what happened to me so you can see how the next series of events proved to me that I was being targeted and they wanted to silence me. I was being falsely accused of a major crime and they were holding me in custody in solitary confinement. My food was being poisoned with arsenic and there was no way a prisoner could bring a chemical such as arsenic to the kitchen where my food was prepared without having access to outside help. You must also be aware of the fact that every conversation is recorded whenever a prisoner calls anyone outside of the prison so you can rest assured if a prisoner tried to get arsenic, the DOC knew about it. Someone was poisoning me and the state police decided that my claim had no merit. They were in collusion against me and what was being totally ignored was the fact that a doctor, not me, but a doctor made it clear based on lab test results that my blood contained high levels of arsenic which was poisoning my body and yet this woman believed my claim had no merit. Her belief had no merit and I was on a mission to prove it someday.

Chapter 7
They Wanted To Silence Me Right From The Beginning

I had gotten shipped out from Lapeer to another facility. I arrived at Adrian facility in 1995. While there I met an officer named Lisa. She was a white woman. We got to know each other very well and eventually formed a good friendship. This didn't sit well with white inmates or other officers. For starters, I was a prisoner befriending an officer and that was not allowed. With her being white, that made it even worse. Soon our friendship turned into something more as we developed a discreet relationship. Everyone knew about it but we basically denied anything so as to protect her job and our lives for that matter. That protection lasted a short stint because something happened to her on one crazy day that led to what I believe was a deliberate plot against my life. I happened on August 13, 1995.

A riot at the prison broke out because the prisoners in the higher floor levels of the facility were angry the they had been taking their yard time away from them. You see, yard time meant time away from the cell and so when they were constantly being denied that time, they became distraught which eventually turned into anger. Apparently they had planned a revolt. They waited for the right day and right time and then launched their attack. The guards blew the emergency siren. I was in the weight room at that time. Once that siren is blown, everyone was obligated to return back to their cell. By the time I arrived back at my cell block, it was in flames and there was fighting going on everywhere. The prisoners and guards were going at it and there was chaos everywhere you turned.

As I was trying to make my way to my cell, I noticed a person laying down unconscious. Immediately I said to myself, hold up, what the fuck? It was Lisa on the floor. They had beaten her and threw a microwave on her. I immediately dropped down to check her vitals. She was still alive but unconscious. Keep in mind that the area we were in was aflame and I had to get her to safety. I remember being upset because nobody even tried to help her including the other guards. I wondered how many people had walked past her while she laid there dying. The attitude of the prisoners was: its us against them. Realizing that fact, I pulled her into an adjacent closet and then pulled her distress button. There were 24 officers who were on duty at the time of the riot. Twelve other officers had been wounded. Seven of them were critically injured.

Eventually outside help was sent to the prison and the riot was brought under control. Luckily Lisa made a full recovery from her injuries. She wrote a memo to the warden and director of the prison stating that I had saved her. She had been hit in the head and stabbed and they had thrown a microwave onto her head. The memo leaked out to the prisoners and in particular, the Aryan nation which is a white supremacist group. The administration knew I saved her life and didn't mention this in any of my transfers whenever I was sent to other prisons. This would have alerted the officials on how to protect me since I saved an officer. She said in that memo that it takes a special person to put their life on the line to save anyone and in this case, he saved me.

Soon I began to notice that I was being treated much differently than at the other prisons I had been to. I still kept helping inmates with their cases however. I spent more time in the law library trying to use that knowledge to help myself and my fellow inmates. I stayed focused and locked and loaded ready to learn. At that point I was starting to win more cases than ever. I was back on a roll after having lost Tracy. I became the go to guy again and I was loving it. I was the man with all of the legal knowledge and everyone wanted me. I was in high demand again. Now, having all of this knowledge had its eventual consequences. I became a nemesis to the warden and the powers that be. They didn't like what I was doing and needed to put an end to it but they knew they had no legal basis. They were literally implementing a protocol to basically undermine me and my efforts to help the inmates and sought out to damage my operation.

As I stated before, I needed this as much as the inmates needed me. I had a new-found purpose and I wasn't about to let them take from me that one thing in prison that brought me a sense of sanity and sense of control. Now, throughout my tenure in prison and in particular, as I had started learning law, injustices started to become more noticeable to me. I started to be more vocal against what the system was doing to us. We had so many unfair treatments that rose to the legal level of inhumane treatment. They kept the joint freezing cold in the winter and gave us the thinnest blankets possible. In the summer, they wouldn't turn the air on often times and so it felt like a furnace up in there. They often denied us access to paper to write our grievances which was a deterrent tactic designed to cause us to just forget about our complaints and accept what they were doing up in there to us. They didn't count on running into a man such as myself who was determined to get justice for me and my fellow inmates. My vigilance would eventually nearly cost me my life on multiple occasions. I always believed they wanted me silenced from the beginning and that belief became clear one hot day in 2010.

On June 12, 2010, I went to the prison yard to run my daily miles. As I was coming back from the yard I began to go up the stairs which led to the floor where my cell was. A dude named Derick was coming back also as I made it to the second floor. The floor I was heading to was on the 4th floor. As I walked up the stairs a guy who rapidly came from out of nowhere rushed up to me and was trying to grab my throat area. He positioned himself in between me and Derick. This was a guy who I had never seen before and had never done any time with during my incarceration. He continued to violently attack me. He grabbed me by the top of my head while still trying to get his hands on my throat. My momentum took me up the steps while he was trying to pull me down the steps.

Then I felt something sharp on the side of my face and I tried to pull away. I realized at that moment that he was slashing my ear and cutting all the way down my face on the right side. I felt disorientated and began to get dizzy. Although, I felt him slashing my ear, I really did not know the full extent to which I was cut. It turned out to be more severe than what I could have imagined. I grimaced in pain and said, "What the fuck!" as I turned around to see who had just stabbed me. What I saw was a big white guy who weighed approximately 300-350 lbs. I did not see his face because when I finally was able to turn around to defend myself, all I saw was was his huge white frame running away. I began to chase to him while still in severe pain. I noticed other prisoners pointing in the direction of my attacker. By this time one of the officers came across my path to intercept me. I looked down at my white T-shirt and it was saturated in blood. It appeared that I had been stabbed at least 5-6 times in my chest and face. The officer noticed all the other prisoners were standing there looking startled, so he called for backup. He ordered me to come forward in his direction. I began to walk towards him. I was about 10-15 feet away from the officer's desk as I began to obey his orders. While walking toward him, I began to feel faint.

I noticed that the officer had started to unravel a fresh roll of toilet paper. He stopped for a moment and put on a pair of rubber gloves. He took the toilet paper and put it on the side of my face and told me to hold it on my face and put pressure on it. By this time 6-7 officers and the sergeant on duty were making their way toward me. I became weaker as I felt that I was about to lose consciousness. I grabbed the roll of toilet paper and put pressure on the side of my face to try and stop the bleeding just as the officer had suggested but to no avail. So, the officer decided to help. He took the toilet paper away from me and then he pressed it real hard on the side of my face to stop the bleeding. By this time the sergeant and other officers began looking for my attacker.

They ran towards one side of the hallway which was the wrong side. They followed that direction because the other prisoners looked in that direction which falsely gave indication as to where my attacker was. That is how prisoners protect each other and protect themselves from being labeled as snitches. The sergeant ordered me to be taken to the prison infirmary. Although, I was on the second floor when this happened, the prison infirmary was in another building. That building was about 100 yards away from where this attack took place which is the length of a football field. They did not provide me with a gurney or wheelchair. They ordered me to walk there even though I was visibly disorientated and about to faint from loss of blood.

There were two officers who escorted me to the infirmary. One of them began speaking on his radio talking to the infirmary saying, "We have one coming and do not know if he will make it." I later found out that an artery was cut and being that I was so inflamed with anger, anxiety and so many emotional whirlwinds, it caused blood to pump even faster. That explained why I had lost so much blood. I still could not get my mind off the fact that I was not placed onto a stretcher or at least helped by the officers on my journey to the infirmary. I was losing all of that blood, dizzy as can be, about to faint and nobody gave a shit but me about my life and whether I would live or die. Upon arriving at the infirmary, I was attended by 2 nurses and met with Lieutenant Johnston. He instructed his sergeant and subordinates to arrange to send me to the hospital.

Before these officers took me, they had to follow protocol to prepare for the ride. They had to go and get their guns and other tactical weapons needed to take prisoners off the grounds. In the meantime, the lead nurse Carol Bennett, was pleading with Lieutenant Johnston trying to convince him to get me to the hospital immediately. In a hysterical voice she yelled, "Please sir, please we got to get him out of here now. He is going to die!" As they were applying first aid to my ear and face, she grabbed a pair of scissors and cut my shirt open to see if there were anymore wounds. The Lieutenant was taking pictures of my injuries. This was taking too much time (2-3 min) as I was continuing to lose so much blood and I was fading in and out of consciousness.

As I continued to fade in and out, I remember hearing Mrs. Bennett talking to Lieutenant Johnston saying, "how long until the ambulance will be here." He replied, "It shouldn't be much longer." He also instructed one of his subordinates to get a prison uniform as it states in the policy of that facility that no prisoner can leave without a uniform. By this time, Ms. Bennett had taken a huge bag of gauze and opened it up and applied it to the side of my face. She said to the other nurse,"Oh my God I can see clear inside of his jawbone!" She then took several ace bandages and rolls of gauze and began to wrap my face with it. By this time the ambulance had arrived and the EMTs were coming through the prison hallway toward me. I heard Ms. Bennett once again yelling loudly, "Please take him out of here, he is dying!" They began strapping me to the gurney.

Ms Bennett continued pleading for my life. Then I heard one of the officers say, "I don't think he is going to make it." That was the second time within 10 minutes that this was said by an officer. After they had securely strapped onto the gurney, they wheeled me into the ambulance and armed guards boarded the ambulance with me. Lieutenant Johnston rode in his car and followed the ambulance to the hospital. Little did I not know at the time that the second car was following the ambulance because they had broken protocol by not having me shackled. They have to follow this protocol to protect themselves and the rest of the inmates and staff.

I had two angels that day. One came in the form of Ms. Carol Bennett who begged for my life. Luckily, the hospital was not that far away. Once I made it to the ER then the guards handcuffed me to the gurney. A team of doctors and nurses helped me into a room and unwrapped my bandages. The doctor who treated me was of Middle Eastern or Indian origin. After removing the last piece of gauze, he looked at the other doctors and started talking to them. I heard him tell the other doctor "I need you to call the Sparrow General Hospital." This hospital was approximately 20-25 min away. The doctor told them that their hospital was not equipped to provide a patient with the appropriate surgeries that was needed. They placed me back in the ambulance and headed to Sparrow Hospital. When we got there, once again, there was a team of staff waiting on us. They immediately rushed me into an already prepared room. The doctor came in and looked at me assessing my injuries.

Then the doctor looked at me and said, "Sir, do you believe in God?" I said, "Yes, Sir!" He said, "We are going to need to pray because I am not a plastic surgeon." He said, "However, God will get us through it!" He was the second angel sent to me that day. He began to order the ER staff to prepare for the emergency surgery to repair the arteries under my left earlobe. They discovered that 2 arteries were split. He ordered the trauma team to assist him in the surgery. After repairing the arteries, he began to close my face. He had to sew my ear back together because it had been slashed in half. There were a total of 37 stitches to my face and neck area towards my juggler. I later found out his name was Dr. Estate. After the surgery was completed, he said to me, "We're done. Would you like to take a look at it?" I said yes. He asked the ER nurse to give me a mirror out of the drawer. I remember watching as everyone in the ER room including the guards that were there to secure me were looking at me as I peered into the mirror. They all said to me, "You look good, MR. Moore, you look good." In my mind I couldn't imagine myself looking good at all because of what just happened to me.

Before the surgery, all I kept hearing were words such as his face had been torn open. I heard adjectives such as disfigured being used to describe me. So in my mind, there was no way that I could believe that I looked good. I held the mirror with my right hand, and I pulled it towards my face. When I looked into the mirror, I shook uncontrollably. I could not believe that was me. My whole right side of my face was pulled together in bunches of little knots where the stitches were placed. I felt pain from the top of my head all the way down my neck as I made expressions with my face. I was not horrified by what I saw, but saddened to the point of pure disbelief.

Tears began running down my face and my nose began to drip from the flowing stream of mucus. Even though they saved my ear, I still couldn't figure out where I looked good at. What was good about this I asked myself? I did not want to offend anyone of then for all the efforts they made to save my life by showing displeasure in the work they did on me, so I said, "Good job." The doctor ordered that my face be wrapped and released me back into the custody and care of the prison facility with the instructions for the doctors at the prison to attend to my injury 3 times per day by changing the gauze and applying ointment to my face.

I was taken to the Prison and escorted back to my cell. Later that evening, I was seen by prison officials including healthcare staff. I was informed that I would not be going back into general population even though they had apprehended my attacker. For pain, they gave me regular Tylenol and Motrin. I needed something stronger but because they considered prisoners as second class citizens, we did not get the best treatments or medications. This went on for 3-4 days and then I was told by prison officials that I would be transferred. Little did I know at that time that the transfer would be a punishment instead of a way of protecting me. They sent me to Marquette, Michigan up in the northern peninsula of the state. My face was still bandaged as I was being transported. I was supposed to be given a medical stay because no prisoner should be transferred when they are under the care of doctors. However, I was not given those basic rights. They had other plans which began to manifest itself to me clearly. I started feeling that somebody wanted me dead.

My brother Ralph started asking about the investigation into the attempted murder of my life or whether there was even an investigation happening at all for that matter. In my humbled opinion, I believe this caused them to view me and my family as trouble makers for the system to have to deal with. We couldn't be silent and walk away accepting what happened. Instead we were making trouble for them by wanting external investigations. I believe I was sent up north because by sending me to the furthest facility away from family and friends, they were hoping that would deter me from seeking justice.

What they didn't know about me was the fact that I was not going to be deterred from getting justice. I hadn't been writing all of those articles about injustices, studying law, helping my fellow inmates beat their cases, writing politicians and contacting lawyers for amusement. I wanted to be heard and so I was not going to go away silently without a fight. I made it to Marquette Branch Prison with my face still swollen and in bandages. To theirs and my surprise my family came to see me within the first week of arrival up north. At that visit my face was still bandaged. Mama and Ralph asked me what could they do to help me. Now because I started believing that someone on the inside of the prison system wanted me dead, I told my brother to call the FBI.

I had been convinced in my mind that they were trying to kill me. It was more than just a figment of my imagination. Their actions were a constant affirmation that they wanted me eliminated and not just my voice silenced. I was an enemy to them because I was helping people win their cases and helping some of them get out of prison and finally go home. You have to understand that they make money off of each prisoner. They are paid thousands upon thousands of dollars a year just for one prisoner. I was taking their profit away from them by helping people get out of prison. All I was doing was helping these people receive the justice they deserved and which was promised to all of us by the founding fathers of our country. Little did I know that this justice I was bringing to them had been slowing becoming my enemy the whole time. Keep in mind that on multiple occasions, they had already told me that I was going to die in there because I was never going to ever get out.

Prior to coming to this facility, my security level had been lowered to level one which is minimum security and now all of a sudden they raise me back up to maximum security without having any tickets or disciplinary action done to me to justify the status change. I must also mention the fact that prior to my speaking out against the system, I had only been transferred to another prison twice. Then afterward, they kept shipping me all across the state of Michigan. I ended of serving part of my prison time in 32 different facilities. It doesn't take a rocket scientist to figure out what was happening. They didn't want me staying at a facility for any great length of time to prevent me from establishing any allies, friends or affording me the opportunity to help anyone. They wanted to silence me from that moment on.

Chapter 8
Divine Intervention

I was sent to general population instead of going to a protection unit. I stayed at that prison for several months. Then on Easter Sunday I was stabbed again. I was assigned to go the gym. On that particular day upon arrival at the gym, there were no guards waiting to acknowledge my presence. This particular assignment was not my normal gym assignment day and I felt apprehensive but I wisely knew I couldn't disobey the assignment directive. In a maximum security setting, we always had to be chaperoned to and from an assignment and no guards escorted me to the gym which was unusual. It was well known throughout the prison that I could play chess well, so some guys asked me if I wanted to play. I said, "yes." I began to play chess with some dude I had never seen before.

As the game was being played, it was my turn to move and so I reached my arm out to grab my pawn to move it. As my hand was outstretched to move my pawn, the guy to my right was also reaching his had out but only to stab me in my right eye. He used a long-sharpened pencil. I was right handed and so I was using my right hand to move my pawn. He sat to my right and reached over and shoved that pencil in my right eye. I yelled out in a loud tone as I was experiencing excruciating pain. As I am sitting on the bench my feet and legs were under the bench. I fell to the floor to keep him from stabbing me. He followed me to the floor. The pencil was lodged deep into my eye and he kept punching me in that eye so that the pencil would go all the way in. I felt my whole eyeball pop out.

During all of this commotion, there were no guards in sight. I tried to cover my face up and my instincts kicked in telling me that if I was going to live then I had to save myself. I covered myself by sticking my arms up over my head. I could not believe that were no guards to come and save my life. Although my pain was intense and I was losing blood and couldn't see, I began throwing blows at my assailant. Since I had never met this man which meant I had no particular beef

121

with him, it led me to believe someone sent him there deliberately and that explained why there were no guards. I had sensed that they wanted me dead and it was becoming more clear to me now at that point. The other men at the table began throwing blows at me. They were kicking me in the head and I was steady losing consciousness.

As I was about to lose consciousness I distinctly remember faintly hearing what I believed was one of the guards coming toward us saying, "No, no that is enough!" Then I passed out. Then the guards used smelling salts to awaken me. I had suffered tremendously. I had a detached optical nerve and my legs felt motionless being weakened by the loss of so much blood. I was brought to my feet by two guards and once again was told to walk to the infirmary. Can you imagine that? My eye was torn out of it's socket and I felt it dangling down my face and these inhumane bastards made me walk to the infirmary even though they had just used smelling salts to awaken me after I had just passed out.

I walked all the way to the infirmary in severe pain with blood still gushing from my eye and when I arrived, a nurse took one look and immediately said, "we got to get him some outside help. He needs to go to the hospital. We can't save him, we can't save him with his eye like this". They rushed me out to Marquette general hospital. They sent me with 4 guards. I was so angry. Now you wanna send 4 guards with me but where were those 4 guards when I was being attacked? An ophthalmologist specialist was called in to assess my situation. She determined that they could not do anything for me and said they need to get me down state to the Ann Arbor Michigan. She placed my eye into a Styrofoam cup to protect it from infection. Keep in mind that this was on Easter Sunday. She had to get an approval from the department of Correction and it is rare that they give approvals on Sundays and this was a holiday as well.

By an act of God, she got the approval and they transported me. When I arrived at the hospital escorted by prison guards, there were a team of surgeons and specialists waiting on our arrival. I met a doctor there named Brian Lee. He is a world famous doctor. He looked at me and said, " I don't know why anyone would do this to you but I want you to know I'm going to save your eye." I was in so much pain and my eye was in a cup and I was bleeding everywhere and so it was hard for me to process the confidence this surgeon had in his own abilities. They had to wait until the swelling in my face went down. What he did for me was nothing short of a miracle. The first surgery was a laser surgery to stop the bleeding and to clean the blood and calluses off of my retina.

I was in recovery for 5 days after the first surgery. He came to me on the 5th day and consulted with me about my condition. He told me he couldn't do anything else at that point until the swelling went down. My left eye was over compensating its usage in place of my other eye. I had nerve damage and my face and brain were still swollen. Attaching my optical nerve back would have helped take the stress off of the other eye but he couldn't perform that procedure until the swelling went down. He sent me back to the prison with direct orders that I was to be moved to a prison hospital called Dewayne Waters Hospital. This facility was approved by the DOC and was one of the first options prisons used when patients needed special care or extended care. Now, tell me why they sent me back to a regular prison instead. I arrived there at 7 pm that night with my entire head still wrapped in bandage.

On April 28, 2011 I was shipped to the Jackson Correction Facility. I was being sent to a maximum security facility. Upon arrival, I was seen by the warden and her deputies to let me know that my life was in danger. They were briefed about my situation and the attacks. They assured me no attacks would happen at their facility. She said to me, "we are going to protect you and make sure that we meet your needs." I was given another affirmation by her that nothing would happen to me again. I don't know why she felt the need to repeat it. She told me that I would only be there until more bed space at the medical facility in Jackson would become available. At 3:26pm, the next day I was summoned by the guards. They informed me again that my life was in danger. I needed to have them assure to me that it was safe for me in that facility. I wanted to hear them say those words. They told me that nothing is going to happen to me and that I was perfectly safe. They sent me back to my room.

At 8:30pm I was supposed to be taken to the infirmary to have my bandage changed again and then afterward I was going to be taken to see the warden again. Keep in mind that at this time of night all prisoners are supposed to be in their cells on lock-down and so no one should be out except porters or people who are seeking medical attention or who work in certain areas. They summoned me to the waiting area which leads to the infirmary. While waiting for the officers to escort me to the prison infirmary, I heard a clicking sound as if someone had locked or unlocked a door and I did not think anything of it because my face was still swollen and all I had on my mind was the pain and the desperate need to get rid of it. Another prisoner's door opened adjacent to where I was standing. Then suddenly one of the prisoners came up from behind me as I was walking out of the door.

He began to stab me with an ice pick in the back of my neck. I went into defense mode and inadvertently, I turned in the direction of where the attack was occurring and my right eye which had already been wounded was exposed. He knew that my eye was already wounded and stabbed me in that same eye. I began to yell out for someone to help me. I was already in so much pain and now I was being stabbed again. I yelled so hard that the guards heard me this time. He lunged at me and punched me in the already injured eye. He saw the guards racing toward us. He heard them yelling Code Red but he did seem to not care. He knew he was an implant. He was the one who attacked me before. I need you to consider and understand something. There were 52 prisons at that time in the state of Michigan. Out of 52 prisons in the state of Michigan, what are the chances of a person being sent to the same prison where an inmate who had previously tried to kill them was being held? I can tell you. The chances are slim and none because it is against the law to send a person to the same facility where a former attacker against them is being held yet, they chose to send me to the same one as my previous attacker.

It was more than just a mere coincidence that he was placed at the same facility, same unit and same side where I was being held. I believe they deliberately placed him there and had him waiting on my arrival so he could ambush me but God had something planned for me. This man who stabbed me before was at this very same prison and I was determined to find out why. How in the world did he end up at the same prison with me? I needed to know who gave that order for him to be sent there while I was being held there. I had been sent up north to Marquette Michigan and then to Ann Arbor and they sent me to the prison with this man who wants me dead? Are you serious? That was how they welcomed me from the hospital. They welcomed me with open arms to another stabbing trying to finish murdering me. Do you understand the legal magnitude of what they were doing to me? They put me in the same prison, on the same floor, on the same cell block with the same man who tried to kill me and placed him 6 doors down from me. I had no doubts in my mind they were trying to kill me.

The officers rushed in and separated us. They took me to the infirmary and handcuffed me to the bed. I had a stab wound to the back of the neck and a puncture wound to the same eye I had just been treated for and there I laid handcuffed to the prison infirmary bed. Where on earth did they think I was going to run to in that condition? My life was on the line and they had me chained to the bed as if I were a wild animal. I was in so much pain and even worse than that, I was boiled over with anger beyond what can be measured because they put me in a position I should not have been in.

The doctor that was on staff looked at me and then turned toward one of the nurses in the room and said, I can not understand why someone wanted to kill him." The Correctional Officer who was in the room then said, "He knows why?" As I am hearing this arrogant officer say this, my face tightened up as I felt anguish and anger. This officer obviously knew nothing about me but yet, there he was posting judgments as if to imply I did something wrong which was causing the attacks. They came toward me and asked me why did I think those people wanted to kill me? I told them that they know the answer already as I looked at the officer.

I asked them why are they asking me such a dumb ass question when they know what is really going on. It was so obvious. There were other prisons they could have sent me to and yet they sent me to the same prison with the same person who had tried to kill me and yet they had the nerve to ask me why? Put yourselves in my shoes and ask yourselves, wouldn't you be pissed off at that point listening to those bogus questions? They should never have sent me back to the same prison where I was injured before. That makes no logical sense. They were sending me back to my would be assailant. How intelligent is that? I told them that they get paid millions of taxpayers money to run the prison system and so they are supposed to know why. I said to them with an emphatic stern voice, y'all are deliberately putting me in these situations. Y'all are creating these situations and you are sitting up here asking me why? I then said, the only thing you can do for me is open up these doors and let me go or be prepared to bury me because that's what your end game is in the first place. You want me dead. You tell the director of the DOC that's what I said. One of them said to me, "you know we can't tell them that. Then I replied saying, then don't waste my time then. Stop talking to me and leave me alone.

Soon afterward, they determined that I needed to go to Foots Hospital in Jackson, Michigan. When we arrived at the hospital, a team of doctors looked at my face and determined that they could not help. Keep in mind that because I was under the care of University of Michigan, I could not have surgery until the swelling had gone down and yet there I was arriving again at another hospital with a new wound on the same eye. They instructed the Correction officers that I needed to be sent back to University of Michigan. They drove me back to the University of Michigan Hospital.

I was in pain the whole time and those wicked bastards did not give me anything for my pain. I arrived at the ER and it seemed like the same people who were on staff when I arrived 4 days earlier were on staff that night also. Dr. Brian Lee was also there as well. While they were escorting me into the ER, one of the nurses on staff recognized me from 4 days before and yelled out saying, "Oh my God he's back!" She saw the new wounds on my face and neck and began to cry. I could hear other staff members saying, "Oh My God, they are trying to kill that poor man up in there." One of them asked me why do they keep doing this to to me. I told her that I did not know why.

She said, "those prison guards need to protect you." Dr. Brian Lee came in and assessed the new damage. I was given another X-ray and CAT Scan. It was determined that the would be assailant who attacked me had ruptured the already detached optical nerve which occurred in the first attack a few days earlier. Then sadly, Dr. Lee had to break even more bad news to me. He informed me that because of the new injuries, he might not be able to save my eye. Uncontrolled tears began to run down my face burning my already wounded eyes. I didn't even consider how painful it was to cry because my heart was injured more than my eyes and I just wanted to see again. It was at that very moment that I spoke to God internally while the Doctor was talking to the staff giving them instructions. I said to God, You have blessed me to see for 44 years. I was able to see beautiful flowers and skies and that was Your will. I feel that You must have a purpose for me because You kept me alive! I don't want to lose my sight Allah, please help me, I don't want to lose my sight. They already took my freedom away from me. Don't let them take my sight away Allah, please don't let them do that to me.

Since my face was swollen, once again, the doctor could not treat me and they sent me back to the prison facility. I was being sent back to the same exact prison where I had just been attacked and yet the warden told me personally that I would be safe there? How safe was I before when they promised me that nothing would happen to me on their watch? I felt they were insulting my intelligence and making a mockery of the situation. This was not a joke to me. I became angered because all of their actions was leading me to believe they had no intention on protecting me and that they seriously wanted me dead.

When I arrived back at the facility, I was not humble but instead, I was irate. I was livid. I wanted those people to hear my pain, and understand my frustration. I wanted to leave no doubt in their minds that I saw them for who they were based on their actions and that someday through the court system, there would be consequences for all of the people who were involved in this conspiracy to take my life. I was put into segregation this time for protection as they had claimed. I asked to speak to the warden, and they said the warden had left for the day. I yelled at the captain and deputy saying, I don't care what it takes, I need to see the warden now. She told me that y'all were going to protect me. Y'all are not protecting me. Y'all are trying to kill me. Y'all are going to pay for this, all of you, I promise you that.

After waiting a few weeks while continuing to remain boiled over in anger, finally, my swelling had went down enough to have the surgeries needed to hopefully restore my vision. I was transported back to the University of Michigan where the surgery was performed. Thank God I was finally in a hospital receiving pain medication and compassion instead of that evil prison that did not give a damn about me. After the surgeries were completed, I laid in recovery uncertain about what was going to happen now. I wondered if my vision could be restored. I wondered where were they going to send me next? I needed protection and I was not getting it from them so I tried to understand what did I need to do to get someone to hear my cries for help.

Although I received the surgeries in prison, I still needed more surgeries and to this day, I have not received all of the necessary surgeries to completely correct my vision and stop the intense headaches I suffer constantly. To open my lens they put a rubber band in my eye to assist my eye. The rubber band wears out eventually and I have constant difficulty seeing. Currently, the state refuses to pay for the surgeries to correct my blindness. After I recovered from the surgeries done at the University of Michigan, I was sent back to the Jackson facility.

I hated going back there because I felt certain in my belief that it was obvious that it wasn't just that particular prison that was in on this conspiracy to kill me. I believed right then and there that this conspiracy extended higher up in ranks all the way up leading to the high ranking officials within the DOC. I knew that somehow, someway, I needed to get in contact with someone on the federal level to help me but that would prove to be a difficult endeavor. While in segregation, because I had yelled at the officers and threatened to sue them, they threatened me and punished me until my eventual release. By law, they have to provide prisoners with paper and pencil and 24 hour access to an attorney but I was not being given any of those rights which is a clear violation of my constitutional right of due process.

My family members were notified of my recent injuries and hospital visits. They were devastated and angered but felt helpless. It was breaking mama's heart and neither she nor Ralph knew what to do or who they should contact to help me get protection. I hated the fact that mama knew what was going on because for 27 years she was basically suffering this prison sentence with me. She didn't deserve none of this pain. I started to doubt whether I would make it out of prison alive. I didn't want to die in prison but all hope was fading and someone with all the power who from behind the scenes was calling the shots. It seemed to me that they were doing everything in their power to make sure I was always in the right place at the right time to be attacked. I had survived some of the cruelest things that could happen behind prison walls and I kept getting denied parole.

I started to put two and two together realizing that they kept denying me parole just so they can keep me in long enough for them to finish trying to murder me. I was at my wits end. I needed someone with a compassionate heart to intervene and help me. The whole time while I was going through all of this, they did not give me an ounce of pain medication and so I had to lay there with my body all stabbed and my eye ripped out and blood dripping everywhere without any medicine to give me any sense of comfort. My brain was swollen and my heart was weighed with a heavy burden of uncertainty and fear. I cried out to Allah. I told Him I don't want to die like this. I promised Him that if He saved me from my oppressors, I would fight so hard and dedicate my life to making sure this doesn't ever happen to another prisoner again.

I started writing grievances against them. You see, they didn't calculate on how determined I was. I was resolved in my belief that I was not going to die in there. My faith in God began to increase. I did not want them to see me looking lethargic and defeated. I wanted them to know they were dealing with not only just me but that they were dealing with me and God. They just didn't realize that they picked a fight with the wrong man this time. Somehow though I think they did know because whenever they dealt with me, they came armed in full force with many officers and riot gear and batons out of fear of what I was capable of because I wore my armor badge on my face instead of my chest. They knew from the look I wore that they needed to be prepared for what might happen. My persona made me likable so they knew I had allies. They respected the boundaries but didn't fully understand the magnitude of my anger toward what they had been allowing to happen to me. I was more than ready to do battle and I was ready and willing to bring the whole system down to their knees.

I wrote the state police and recruited the help of my brother Ralph. I told him to call any and every official he could think of. I said to him, big bro, I want you to get on their damn nerves until they do something about this shit because I will not be silenced anymore. My voice will be heard. Ralph got to work immediately using his position at the Flint Police department and started contacting politicians and anybody who would listen. The administrators at the Flint Police department called Ralph in and told him that although they knew that he loved his brother, his efforts to free me was drawing too much fire for their department. State police were calling them and investigating and it was affecting my brother and his job.

He came up to the prison feeling as though he had pretty much exhausted all of the legal angles he could use. He cried during the visit saying, "Maurice, I don't know what else

131

to do." My mother's heart was breaking and we feared she was on the brink of having a nervous breakdown. Instead of falling in despair and going into panic mode, I turned to God. I became even more determined that I needed to bring those bastards to justice. I knew however, that I had to go through this same system who had become my enemy to try and get justice. It was like the fox guarding the hen house. I had to go to my enemy who was trying to kill me and ask them to save my life.

There I was with my life on the line writing a grievance against the same people who were preventing me from writing grievances. That was the proper procedure before I could file a civil lawsuit. I had to first seek administrative remedies and exhaust all of those remedies on that level. I had a lawyer friend who had recently gotten a promotion. President Obama appointed him as a federal judge. I reached out to him. I had been turned down 4 times by the parole board. I went before them again for a 5th time in December of 2011. Once again they turned me down because I refused to admit I committed murder against Mr Wellington. The next time I would be eligible for another parole hearing would be in another 24 months.

It was at that point that I believed they wanted me to die in there. They wouldn't supply me with paper and pencil to write letters to my family or my attorney. That is how they were treating me. Like a dog. I had to ask some dude I didn't even know to get a letter mailed out to my brother for me and that I would have my brother send him some money in return for him helping me. Those were the kind of things I had to do up in there in order to get outside help. They wanted me silenced and they weren't giving me any opportunity to make contact with my brother. I was determined that I was not going to let them win.

One night as I laid in my cell, I began to question why

God was allowing all of the to happen to me. At the same time, I knew I was still alive in spite of all of those attempts on my life. I knew God must have wanted me alive for a divine purpose. I needed answers and so I began to talk to God asking Him exactly what is it that He wanted me to do. Why is He keeping me alive, I asked Him. I laid there staring upward, not necessarily into the ceiling but just upward in deep thought. Then something told me to get up and go to the door. I got up and went to the door and looked out the small window and I saw a porter sweeping the floor. I noticed that there was a small pencil on the floor in the trash he was sweeping so I tried to get his attention. He didn't hear me at first and so I pounded on the window trying to get him to look up. As he was going right past my door, I knew my window of opportunity to get his attention was about to be lost so I hit that glass with all the power I could muster up short of breaking it and finally, he looked up. I pointed to the pencil and said I need that pencil. He nodded as if to say ok, I got you. Then, while using the dust mop, he maneuvered the pencil under my door and continued on his way.

The pencil he gave me was very small and was not sharpened. I had to literally use my teeth to bite away the wood to expose the led. The pencil was so small that I could barely hold it in between my huge fingers to write with. I had to find a way to use it regardless because at that point, my life was literally depending on this small pencil to write what I needed for it to write. Failure was not an option. I had been saving my napkins from the food they had been trying to feed me. I got those napkins out and started writing a letter to my brother Ralph which I wanted him to take to my attorneys to let them know what they were doing to me. The next night I laid there on the bed and went back in deep thought mode.

Suddenly I heard a voice talking. At first I thought the voice was coming from outside of my room but those doors were pretty thick so you really can't hear too much sound from out there. I just ignored it and continued to stay in meditation thinking about my next moves. Then I heard that voice again. It said, "write this down". I looked around the room and asked, "who is in here"? Then that voice said again, "write this down." I said, write what? Then what I believe to be nothing short of a divine miracle happened.

I started writing down certain court cases I had remembered from when I had been studying law. These were not just ordinary cases. These were cases pertaining directly to what they were doing to me. These cases involved failure to protect, laws concerning putting prisoners back in the same prison with people who they had previous altercations with and much more. The Law states that the prison officials were obligated to separate me from my would be assailants but yet, they placed me in the same cell block with my attackers. The courts had already heard similar cases and ruled against the DOC on those issues. I was remembering these cases and wrote them down. I needed to get that information along with my other letter to my brother Ralph immediately. That next day I saw that porter again and gave him the napkins with my letters and court cases on them and asked him to make sure he mailed them out for me. He did exactly that.

Afterward I just laid in my cell peering at the walls and ceiling. I began reflecting back on all that had happened to me since the day I walked up to my front door to see what Sherry wanted on the day that Mr. Wellington was killed. 27 years had gone by and there I was laying in a bed in a prison in a fight for my life and all because I chose to get out of bed and open a door my beloved Tracy begged me not to open. I thought about every stab wound. Every memory was playing in my mind like a video tape. In my mind I went over step by step the events leading up to each stabbing trying to understand what could I had possibly done to anger anyone to cause them to want me dead. I seriously needed to know the answer and the more I reflected back, I became convinced that the only enemies I had up in there who could possibly want me dead were the people I kept filing grievances against.

These were the same people who didn't want me to help inmates get out of prison. I was a legal threat to their system. I became a political enemy to them. I became a legal adversary and I was certain beyond any doubts they were trying to kill me and I needed to do something immediately or I was going to lose my life. I was determined to live. Mama Henry started calling politicians on my behalf. This 80 something year old woman would go all the way to Lansing, Michigan demanding to speak to somebody in a position of power so that she could inform them of what was happening to me. My brother reached out to one of his colleagues who had received a promotion and was working in Washington. At the same time, I had made contact with my lawyer friend who had been promoted by President Obama"s Administration. I was trying to recruit all of the help I could get using all resources available.

I had just seen the Michigan parole board in December of 2011. Remember that they gave me a continuation which meant I had gotten rejected and had to stay in prison. My determination did not waiver however because I was more than ready to put up a good fight and die fighting if that was God's will. Then finally I received a visit from Ralph. He said, "Maurice, I got your letter man, what do you want me to do?" I said Ralph, you got to make contact with this lady who I had been corresponding with. She's a lawyer from the state ombudsman office. Her name is Jennifer Dunham. I got her ear right now Ralph. She believes me when I tell her that they are trying to kill me. Get in contact with her and tell her I said I need for her to come up here to the prison and see me as soon as possible, do you hear me? He said, "I'm on it bro. I'll contact her right away". My brother drove to Lansing to speak to her and even though she was out in the field visiting multiple prisons all over the state, he waited until she came back to her office. He told her what was happening to me.

That lady came to see me and she said, "I don't know what I can do because this is bigger than both of us. She told me they had a special file on me in Lansing, Michigan. She had the power to go to the central office of the DOC. While there conducting her inquiry into my case and the allegations I was making against the DOC, she discovered that they had been speaking back and forth with Internal affairs within the Department. She saw emails of them talking back and forth with each other trying to decide where to send me. This is why she told me that what was happening was bigger than me and her. Nonetheless, she was to me an angel sent by God to help me.

This small white Jewish woman with a 5'2" frame said to me, "I'm not going to stand idly by and let them do this to you. I don't care what my bosses say, and I don't care what the Department says. I am going to go to the Federal government and see if I can get you out of this prison because it is obvious they are in fact trying to kill you". Before she had visited me, she had tried to get them to send me to one of the two protection facilities in the state and they refused. She knew then that it was definitely bigger than her or me and she rightfully concluded that we needed the Federal government involved. If any person qualified to be in one of those protection prisons, my situation certainly exceeded theirs and yet I kept being denied protection.

I was being stabbed on a consistent basis and in all cases, there were supposed to be guards there to protect me and yet I was put in predicaments which allowed plenty of time for an assailant to get to me without fear of the guards. Somebody wanted those guards out of their normal routine positions for a reason. I was so thankful that she understood all of this and vowed to help. We begged and begged them to protect me. Mama begged them constantly. She called them frantically scared for her son's life like a loving mother would and yet they ignored her and kept trying to kill her son. Mama Henry begged them to protect me. She sacrificed her health and her money traveling as an elderly woman to government institution after institution trying to get someone to intervene and help me. My brother Ralph begged them to protect me. He put his job and reputation on the line begging them to help me. They had no intention on listening to them or helping me because they wanted me dead. I was convinced of that and now I had an ally, an angel who was equally convinced they wanted me dead too.

My brother had gotten in contact with someone on the Federal level in the Department of Justice. Then one day in early January of 2012, I received a visit from the chairwoman of the Parole board. Keep in mind that one month earlier in December, 2011 I had just went before the parole board and was denied parole and given what is called a 24 month continuation which meant that the next time I would be able to go before them would be in 2 more years. I was already into my 27th year behind bars so as you can see, they very much intended to keep me there for the rest of my life possibly. It is very rare for the Chairman of the Parole board to conduct a hearing but that is what she came there to do on this day. She told me that she was there to personally interview me by the authority of the Federal government. I was totally stunned. Finally, Somebody outside of the Michigan DOC was listening to me and hearing my pleas for help.

This wasn't a normal interview that is typical for a parole hearing. I had to wait an hour before the interview to start. I wanted the deputy warden to attend because I wanted him to hear all of the things that they were doing to me so she could see the look on his face. Once the interview started, she started treating me as if I was the problem. In my mind I was thinking, here we go again. These people don't want justice. I

137

thought she was here to find the truth and bring about justice but instead she talked to me as though I were a perpetrator instead of a victim. I thought for sure that the interview was a bust. I went back into my solemn melancholy and began withdrawing from everything. I remained in solitude as a recluse trying to understand what else could I do to convince these people to set me free.

A few days later, the warden, two of his deputies and one of the captains came to me carrying a piece of paper. The captain was one of the nicer officers who I had known since he was a rookie officer. I had know him for 17 years and watched him climb the ladder from a regular corrections officer all the way up to captain. Now, I had seen so many papers like the one he was about to hand me. Those papers looked exactly like the parole papers I had received 5 times saying denied, denied, denied, denied, denied. I was in no mood to hear that shit anymore. Even through all of those denials, I never lost hope and I never gave up my fight for my freedom. I stood there in front of them with no expectations of anything good and had already hardened my heart against the rejection I had been prepared for.

I grabbed that paper from the warden and read it. I looked at the warden and said, what kind of a sick ass joke is this? He said, "no, Moore, its for real." I looked at that paper again. It was dated January 15, 2012. At the top of the page it said, "From the United States Department of Justice". Underneath that it read "Michigan Department Of Corrections (DOC)". Then the next line said, "SPECIAL PAROLE". I continued to read on. It said, "You have since been on this day paroled/pardoned by the DOC, State of Michigan EFFETIVE on January 18, 2012". I could not believe my eyes. I did not comprehend immediately the fact I was actually being freed. I still thought this was some kind of cynical joke. The warden then asked me if I would like to go and make a phone call to alert my family? I said, is this for real or is this a joke? The captain who had accompanied the deputies said, "no Moore, it's definitely real. I'm going to make sure that I be there in the morning with you when they release you. Congratulations man, you're finally going home." That's when I started to believe this is might really happening. My heart began racing so fast. I still couldn't fully believe it though I desperately wanted to. Am I a free man? Am I really a free man, I kept asking myself?

The warden escorted me to his office and I made that phone call. I called my mother. She had been waiting on this moment for 27 years. She answered the phone and I said, Ma, are you ready for some good news? Mama said, "boy I could sure use some good news right now." I said, ma, they set me free. She said, "what are you talking about baby." I said mama, Obama and them let me go. I've been paroled. I don't know what happened on the other end to mama, but one of my nephews grabbed the phone. He was so excited. I said to him, nephew, I'm free. They let me go. I'm coming home. Eventually after collecting herself after having been told such great news, mama got back on the phone. I told her to tell my nephew Ty'rome to bring me up me up some clothes to wear when I am released.

I went back to my cell and yet somehow, reality hadn't fully sunk in that I was in fact going home. I had fought 27 years for this moment and now I struggled to believe it was actually happening. I had survived so many attempts against my life and being alive was a blessing but I wanted more. I wanted to be free. My will and determination to be free was even greater than my will to just survive. It was far superior over their will to kill me. I kept remembering what Allah said in Quran in surah 2:287 when He said, "no soul will be burdened beyond its capacity to bear it." I therefore kept reminding myself I could get through this. I had Allah with me all the time. He also said in Quran in Sarah 53:40, "And that man will have nothing but what he strives for." I wanted to live. That is what I strive for everyday. God kept me alive in accordance with His will and in accordance with what He said I can have when I strive for it. I wanted to be free someday and I fought hard to stay alive so that someday I would walk through those iron bars and walk out of that door a free man and I was laying right there in that bed holding papers which contained my freedom.

I laid there in my cell still staring at that letter reflecting on the magnitude of what I was holding in my hand. I thought about my ancestors and how they must have felt when their slave masters set them free. It was as though I was reconnecting with them and holding their freedom papers reliving their triumphant moment. To me, I was holding in my hand more than just my freedom. I was holding the power of my ancestors in my hand. I was holding a symbol of their hope they passed down to me and my people. I was holding a symbol of power far greater than the power the DOC thought they had over me. I was holding proof that I had prevailed over them and their wicked attempt to kill me. I held in my hand proof of what can happen to you if you never give up. I held in my hand proof that Allah has power over all things.

I don't get into religious debate with nobody because every person has some kind of testimony about their own personal experience with what they perceive to be the power of and or presence of God. One thing I can say for certain though is that I have no doubts in my mind that Allah heard my prayers and I believe with all my heart and soul that He protected me by sending to me angels in the form of human beings to help me. I am alive and it is because of Allah and I will believe that until the day life itself ceases to exist.

Chapter 9
Coming Home Finally

On the eve of my release, I was still in a quiet denial wondering if it was all true because I had received 5 denials from the parole board and 9 rejections from the courts for appeal. In my mind, it didn't make sense why this one particular time, it would be true after all of those rejections. Keep in mind that I had just recently been stabbed in my right eye. I read that letter over and over again trying to focus my injured blurry eyes on it to make certain it was really what I was seeing. The warden and his two deputies were standing outside of my cell at that time. I looked through the window of my cell door and asked the warden again if this was really real. He said yes, "Moore, I don't know who it is that you know, but you are being released at 8:00 in the morning."

I couldn't sleep at all that night. I kept doing pushups all night to keep myself occupied. I had told myself that as soon as the morning shift began at 6:00 in the morning, I was going to ask that guard who would be on duty if he had heard any news about my impending release. It was only 3:00 am and time seemed to stand still. I had become worn out from doing all those pushups and so I began to pace back and forth in my cell for the next 3 hours. I was exhausted but sleep was not an option because I didn't want to fall asleep and then wake up only to find out this had all been a dream.

At 6:05 that morning I heard a guard walking toward me as his keys were jingling. My heart started pounding faster and faster. He was doing his normal rounds walking throughout the cell block. I was standing right at my window as he approached my door. Before I could even ask him if he had heard anything about my release, he said, "congratulations Moore. Do you need anything before you leave such as a shower or some breakfast?" I looked him in the eyes and said I'm straight on the food but I would like to have that shower. He said, "when I get back up front, I will open your cell so you can take a shower. If you need anything else just let me know ok."

Within in a few minutes afterward, the cell door opened up. Now, normally when a prisoner is in segregation, they are led to and from their cells in handcuffs. When my door opened and they came to escort me out, I was not placed in handcuffs and this became a good sign for me that this wasn't a dream and that I was really about to go home finally. As I was being escorted to the shower, one of the correction officers asked if I needed soap or shampoo which is customary that they ask if those things are needed to which I replied, yes. I told them I need some soap. I normally would wash my face with my eye patch on but this day I decided to take it off. I took it off because I didn't want it to get wet. I was trying to decide if I wanted to wear it when I walked out of the door because I was self conscious about my eye and how it may appear to others.

I began to wash my face and soap got into my injured eye and I yelled and the guard came rushing into the shower area and said, "whats wrong Moore." Then as I rinsed my eyes with water my vision became more clearer than it had been before. I said to him, I can see you, I can see. He replied saying, "what do you mean?" I said, "man, I can see you moving, this is great man, I can see." He laughed and said, "that's great Moore." Then he left and I kept placing my hand over my left eye so that I can try and see with strictly my right eye to make sure that my vision was really getting better. I'm no doctor but I think at that time, I probably had about 20 % of my vision in that eye.

After I dried off and finished my shower, I put on my blue prison uniform and walked toward the control center. When I arrived, captain Johnston who had told me he would come and see me when they were ready to release me met with me at the control center. He had been promoted to captain. He saw me approaching and he came from outside of the control bubble which is the glass encasement where the guards are stationed. He walked up to me carrying 3 documents containing my release and the conditions of my release. We both stared at each other with a look of joyful relief as he held an ink pen and asked me to sign each section where there was an X.

One of those pieces of paper I needed to sign was a document stating that I could not be around any guns or fire-arms. The other one I signed stated that I agree to follow the conditions of parole which meant that I would have to report to a specified parole officer monthly for 2 years. After I finished signing the paperwork, we looked at each other again and he shook my hand and said, "good luck." I said to him, thank you for always treating me with respect and for treating me like a man. He in turn said to me, "thank you for teaching me how to be a better man and a better correction officer."

He walked with me past the first control station and led me all the way to the third control station. At that point, he went back to his control station. I was standing in between the corridor that separates the prison side from the visitors side. While standing there waiting, my mind began playing tricks on me telling me that someone was going to come through that door and tell me that there had been a mistake and they were releasing the wrong guy. After what seemed like an eternity while waiting in that area behind that door, it finally opened. I walked through it into a lobby filled with family and friends and people who I didn't know such as news reporters and dignitaries, officials from the DOC, politicians and members of clergy.

My nephew Ty'rome appeared from out of the crowd of people and handed me a bag containing clothing. I took the bag and went into the bathroom to change out of that dreadful government issued slave identifying clothing. Once in the bathroom, I opened up the bag and looked at the clothes in amazement that finally, finally I was about to shed that oppressive uniform and wear regular clothes again. It was in the middle of January and so I was given a nice warm heavy black coat with fur around the hood. There was a pair of jeans and some boots and a button down shirt and there was actually a real belt. Now you may be wondering why I said a real belt. You see, in prison, we weren't allowed to have a real belt and so they issued a spandex cloth as a belt to hold our pants up. Having a real belt finally, meant more to me than what most people can ever understand.

I changed into my new clothes and happily threw my old uniform into the trash with an emphatic motion as if to say thank God I don't have to wear that bullshit ever again. I opened the door of that bathroom and began to walk out. As I walked out of that door, I finally began to really feel free. I looked up into that crowd of people and immediately spotted my mother and I walked up to her. Cameras were aimed at me and I could see all of those lights flashing as they were taking pictures. I finally reached mama and hugged her so tight.

I saw that her eyes began to swell up with tears so I held her even tighter and kissed her and said mama, I'm free. I'm free mama, I'm coming home. Then my sister Janice and mama Henry joined us in a group hug and Janice said, "are you ready to go"? I looked at her and said, I was ready to go 27 years ago. She said, "I know." I didn't see Ralph and so I asked where was my brother Ralph. Mama told me that he had to work and couldn't get off. Then I looked around and saw my sister Sherry. That was the first time I had seen her in 27 years. It was so awkward but yet humbling to see her free as well. She cried uncontrollably and said, "bay bay, I am so sorry." I walked up to her and I wrapped my arms around her and said, its ok. Its all behind us now.

She kept saying, "I'm so sorry, I really am sorry." I could tell that she was very nervous and so I clinched her hand to let her know I'm ok with everything and there was no need to carry that heavy burden of guilt anymore. I looked her directly into her eyes and said its ok, its all over and done with. We both are free. We all began to walk towards the front door of the prison as everyone looked on cheering and clapping. The warden came up to me and said, "good luck Mr. Moore" and I looked at the warden and said, you will be hearing from me again. That's when a reporter asked me, "what is one of the first things you are going to do?"

I guess I surprised everyone when I responded by saying I'm going to take a long bath. They all chuckled. What they didn't understand is the fact that for 27 years, I was not able to take a bath. We didn't have bathtubs in prison and so I couldn't wait to finally sit in a tub full of warm water and soapy bubbles and just relax and wash all of that 27 years of prison experience off of my body once and for all. We walked out that door to cars awaiting us as if we were dignitaries being escorted to the White house. We drove to Denny's to have breakfast. The whole entire group who came to the prison accompanied us including 2 of the reporters and some men in suits who I assumed were government officials.

My sister Janice said to me, "you can order anything you want." We all sat down at the table assigned to us by the waitress. What astounded me the most was that I was actually sitting in a restaurant looking at a table that had real silverware. I felt like I was in euphoria because as I had told you previously, we weren't allowed to have silverware. We only used sporks and there I was sitting at a table with real forks and spoons and knives and a menu. Can you imagine how I was feeling? I had an actual menu for the first time in 27 years and was being allowed the opportunity to order anything I wanted. We ordered our food and for the first time in what seemed like forever, I was able to actually enjoy some real food.

Afterward we all met up at mama's house and let me tell you, that house was packed with even more family and friends than what was at the prison. We partied and reminisced all throughout the night. Finally, I got that long awaited bath, It was everything I imagined it would be and then some. It was so therapeutic. Once I finished bathing, it was time to lay my head down and soak all of this in. I had just spent 27 long years of my life behind bars and now I was free. I wondered where do I go from here? What is my next move, I wondered. One thing I knew for sure was that I wanted to bring my oppressors to justice and so it didn't take long for me to get sharpened back up to the level I was at when I was helping so many prisoners win grievances. Now it was my turn to fight my own battles against the system and I was ready to do battle.

Now shortly before I had begun to implement my strategies of how I was going to go about my lawsuit against the DOC, I had gotten myself a job at a bar. I got that job through my brother Ralph who was head of security at that bar establishment as a side job adjacent to his job with the police force. While working there I became friends with one of my coworkers named Amanda. We hit it off very well. She was in college working on her nursing degree. Eventually we decided to start dating. She was very computer savvy and immediately started helping me with everything I needed to do concerning my lawsuit and helped me to organize my files and things like that. I was not only gaining a new woman in my life, I had gained a helper who had organizational skills that became essential to the next chapters of my life. Armed with my passion and determination and now with Amanda by my side, I was ready to take on Goliath.

By April of 2012 after my release from Prison, I had contacted about 13 law firms altogether. One of those law firms happened to be one of the most prominent law firms in Michigan. Now keep in mind that throughout the whole time when I was in prison and especially during the time while I believed my life was in danger, I had been compiling evidence against the DOC and their officials knowing that someday I had planned to file a lawsuit against them regardless if I had to do it a a free man or as a prisoner. I was determined to bring them to justice because I definitely believed beyond any doubt that there was a conspiracy to eliminate me. I believed firmly that they had placed me in harms way purposely and for multiple reasons. One of those reasons was that I had contacted US senator Carl Levin and the Department of Justice to inform them of the wrong doings against the prisoners that the DOC were taking a blind eye to.

Little did I know that in doing so, this same justice system I was petitioning for help would be the very same Justice system that became my enemy as I will explain later in this book. I also contacted an attorney named Allison Oliver who I was referred to by a person I had met through the Michigan State University Law alumni. She has some very wise attorneys in her firm association. Together we decided to embark on this long journey of filing a lawsuit against the State of Michigan and the DOC knowing that both of them had powerful resources and plenty of money to defend themselves.

We were the David going up against the Goliath. Nick Sushi was the first person I spoke to from that firm and after telling him the facts of my story, he immediately knew they were going to take my case. He convinced Ms. Oliver to take my case which was an easy endeavor. The first thing they did was hire investigators to verify the merits of my claims. They followed the proper protocols for filing a federal lawsuit which was to notify the Department of Justice that we were filing a failure to protect, conspiracy and retaliation lawsuit against the State of Michigan, the DOC, the warden at the prison where the stabbings took place and the subordinates under the jurisdiction of the warden who allowed these atrocities to happen.

The reason for the retaliation portion of the lawsuit was

because they repetitively denied me the right to file grievances against them for failure to protect and for trying to poison me to death. By law they were obligated to supply me with paper and pencil and access to the library and the ability to contact an attorney which I was denied access to on all accounts. I had a right to be protected and they failed to do so but instead as stated before, kept putting me in harms way knowingly and deliberately. Congress had previously set these guidelines and each state within the union are mandated under federal law to uphold these guidelines. I was never supposed to be placed back into a prison with someone who had previously tried to take my life.

While my lawsuit was pending, me and Amanda continued to grow in our relationship. I had met some of her family members and she had met mine as well. In between that time, I was of course enjoying my new freedom and started reaching out to old friends from the neighborhood I grew up in. It wasn't hard reconnecting because Flint was so small. Soon, I began to experience what some may call postpartum depression. I had already been having nightmares about those stabbings ever since the stabbings happened. Now they started to become more frequent. It was scaring Amanda. She told me that often, I would awaken and start swinging as if someone was attacking me. She became really concerned about me and felt I needed to get some help. I started seeing a psychiatrist about what I was going through. Then I started getting terrible headaches and I went to see several doctors and they all concurred that the massive headache pain was in direct relation to the damaged nerve in my eye. With all of this pain and postpartum stress, I felt I was about to lose my mind. I was getting tired of all of those doctors appointments and the stress was getting the best of me. My blood pressure began to swell and doctors feared that I would end up having a stroke or heart attack if I didn't do something differently.

Chapter 10
A New Life In Atlanta

I was definitely ready for a change of scenery. I needed to get away. I was so worried that my life was in jeopardy which was causing stress for Amanda. I was at risk of a stroke and I was feeling as though I was putting her health at risk along with mine. If something had happened to her, my whole world would have been crushed. I thought that maybe if I went somewhere else beside Flint, Michigan, then perhaps things would get better for my health which would in turn help my relationship with Amanda because I knew my situation in dealing with those nightmares and everything was indeed affecting her. I reached out to my dear brother in spirit, Salih who I had been told was living in Atlanta. We had a great conversation. He suggested that maybe I should move down there to Atlanta, Georgia and start a new life. It sounded like an excellent idea. I told him I would get back with him on that because I wanted to run it by Amanda and see how she felt about moving. She also felt that it was a great idea so we began making plans to head that way.

Moving became my main priority and Atlanta seemed like a great choice to get away and rebuild. Regardless of where I went, I definitely wanted to get as far away from Flint, Michigan as possible and the more I kept hearing about Atlanta the more I wanted to go there. Moving to Florida or California would have been my first of choices but Atlanta seemed like a temporary consolation prize especially since Salih lived there. I mean, good weather, good economy which meant great opportunities to come up so I definitely took advantage of that golden opportunity. I called Salih back and we talked for a great while reminiscing about how things were back in the day when we were in the joint together. There was much to laugh about and be angry about as re reminisced.

Much of the anger came as I had to tell him about what happened to me during all of that time after he left. As I told my story to him, he interrupted me and told me with excitement that I need to write a book about my life because the world needed to hear my story. I told him that other people had suggested the same thing to me. With that same excitement still resonating in his voice, he stated to me that his older brother Clark had written a book before and he recommended that I should talk to Clark about helping me write my story. He told me that he would reach out to his brother first before he could give out his brother's number without permission. My brother Salih always had that type of etiquette and I could tell that he was definitely the same compassionate person he was when we were together in the joint. He always had such a kind, caring and charitable nature and I could tell by the tone in the sound of his voice that he was willing and would do whatever he could within the confines of his power to help me.

Luckily, Salih was a regional manager at a company which gave him the power to hire people. He told me that he had recently gotten married and that his sister Faye was also living with him. He explained to me that because of those circumstances, he didn't have much room in his house for me and Amanda but that he would reach out to Clark to see if he could allow us to come and stay with him until we could stack up enough money to get our own place. Later on that day he called me back with the greatest news. He informed me that he had indeed talked to Clark and that not only was Clark willing to allow me and Amanda to live with him but that he was not going to charge us for any room and board. He gave me Clark's number and told me to call him and that he was expecting my call. I was so eager to contact him that I hurried up the conversation with Salih so that I could hurry up and call his brother.

I called Clark and he was shaving at the time so I suggested that he could call me back when he was finished but instead, he insisted that he could put his business on hold to accommodate me. He told me that he had indeed been briefed by Salih of my situation and said that he would allow me and

Amanda to live with him and that he would not charge any rent. He only gave one stipulation which was that in exchange for room and board, he wanted us to keep his house clean. I remember thinking to myself, man, you gotta be kidding me. Is this guy for real? Do angels really exist? I mean, this dude was a godsend.

I later found out from Salih that Clark had already said yes that me and Amanda could stay with him before he had even been told about my story or about possibly helping me write the book. He said yes because his brother's friend needed help. Knowing that, it made me feel even more confident about working with Clark. This showed me that he was helping me out of the kindness of his heart and not for any monetary gain or hidden agenda. We talked for a couple of hours that day as I gave him the run down of my life and why I reached out to him for help. He told me about his book that he wrote called "CONVICTING THE WORLD OF SIN" and that he also worked on Neffie's book as well. Neffie is the sister of singer, Keyshia Cole and she was a co-star with her on their Reality TV show. I was sold on having him work with me because he showed his impressive resume. I mean, this dude wrote his own book and helped write a book for a celebrity too. I was overly excited.

Then he told me that he was the original co-founder of a famous legendary R&B from Flint where we grew up at. He also told me that he was now a solo artist working on releasing a song onto the market. I kept thinking to myself as we talked, damn, what can't this guy do? Then to top it all off, while I was telling him my story, he interrupted me and told me that he had already thought of a title for my story. What he told me was nothing short of genius and brilliance and although I knew I had already decided he was going to be my choice to help me write my story, the words which came out of his mouth at that very moment made me know for certain that he was definitely the right man for the job. He said, WHEN

JUSTICE BECOMES THE ENEMY. I laughed so loud with joy and excitement. I mean, wow, this dude was so sharp and perceptive. How did he put the whole story summary together in such a brief conversation with such intimate accuracy to come up with such a brilliant title? That was the only word to describe what came out of his mouth. Just Brilliant. I was ready to get started immediately. The world needed to hear my story. Justice had indeed become my enemy and there could not have been any other title to more appropriately capture my experience and people needed to know exactly how Justice sometimes becomes our enemy.

Now I was even more convinced that I needed to get to Atlanta. I called Salih and thanked him for plugging me in to his brother. Salih came up to Michigan and picked me and Amanda up. I was so excited to see this brother. Words cannot accurately explain what I was feeling. We embraced and man let me tell you, I nearly choked the life out of this brother. That's just how happy I was to see him. He came in and greeted mama and she pretty much did the same exact thing I had just done. She gave him the longest and warmest hug. To mama, Salih was her son too and she was so elated to see him. After visiting for a while reminiscing about our past experiences, it became time to hit the road and head to Atlanta. It was hard having to leave mama, but I needed to get to Atlanta because I had so much I was ready to tackle and accomplish in life. We hit the road.

We talked on the highway and started mapping out what it was that I was going to accomplish. As we traveled, I started looking at all of the beautiful mountains and became so grateful I was now free and and able to bask in God's glorious creation. I was able to look at all of those beautiful sights along the journey even with my impaired vision and so that made the journey even much more pleasurable and it made me even more excited about my big move. As we passed through each major city along the highway, I could feel my intensity level in my adrenaline pumping higher and higher. When we passed through Knoxville, Tennessee I saw the first sign on the highway that said those words I was waiting to see. Atlanta! We were getting close. I couldn't wait to get that ride over with. Finally, we pulled off the highway and were heading toward Clark's house.

As we pulled up into Clark's driveway, I remember thinking to myself, well, we finally made it. That moment has now arrived. My new life begins right now. I was certainly relieved to get off that highway after that long 12 hour drive and my blood was pumping with excitement as we got out of the car and began to grab our luggage out of the trunk. We followed Salih toward the house as we walked up the driveway. Finally after arriving to the door with luggage in tow, I stood there in anticipation wondering what was going to happen next in my new life after that door finally opens. Salih rang the door bell as me and Amanda eagerly stood there. Within what seemed like only a few seconds later, Clark's son Malik came and answered the door and welcomed us in and informed us that his dad was upstairs recording but was expecting us and told us to come right on in. We set our luggage in the foyer area and then me and Amanda both gave Malik the biggest hug as if we were long lost family. Then we followed Malik up the stairs as he led us to the studio room where Clark was recording. He was recording a song called "Sasha" which he was planning to release soon.

When he came out of the vocal recording booth to meet us, we both greeted each other with a strong brotherly hug. He then turned toward his computer and saved what he had just sang on his track and then graciously gave us his undivided attention. He asked us how was our trip and wanted to know if we wanted anything to eat or drink. I assured him that we were just fine and that the trip was long but pleasant. I was more interested in wanting to know more about that song he was singing because I was really digging that song. I asked him who wrote those tracks he was singing. He told me that he wrote all of the music, did all of the production work and all of the vocals all by himself. I was in awe. I said damn' man you did all of that? He said, "yep, all by my lonesome" I said man, you got a gift. You are too talented. He was so humble about it though and shied away from the praise and accolades but I said it anyway because it needed to be said. I mean, this brother is so talented and when I say so talented, I mean gifted in so many ways. I compared him to Jamie Fox who could sing and act. That's how good this brother is. I mean, this brother could sing and write music, write literature, was a talented artist and was basically a religious teacher as well.

Right from the start, Clark made me and Amanda feel right at home. We were given our own private bedroom instead of having to sleep downstairs on the couch. We did sleep on the couch however for a few weeks until we were able to purchase a mattress to sleep on upstairs in the room. We both fell in love with his two little sons named Hunter and Aaediin and their older brother Malik. Malik showed us his skills as a voice actor by doing his Stewie imitation from the character on Family Guy. He is so talented. He really sounded exactly like Stewie. He also did Disney characters such as goofy and Mickey Mouse. Oh, and I can't leave out SpongeBob. He sounds exactly like each one of those characters.

Both of his youngest sons were gifted in mathematics. We would give them math problems to solve and they would solve them without using pencil or paper or a calculator. That Aaediin was something else though. That little kid was only 6 years old but could tell you the answer to 5,467 x 27 and would give you the answer in a matter of seconds and like I said before, he did this without a calculator or pencil and paper. He did that math right in his head and had I not witnessed it myself, I would have not believed it if someone had told me about it. Aaediin and Hunter were really quiet at first but eventually opened up. It just felt like we had known each other forever. Every Friday, due to his work schedule, Clark would conduct Jumah prayer services at his home and being a Muslim myself, naturally I attended. He would give some powerful lectures that rivaled the likes of Malcolm X and Martin Luther King. Sometimes we'd joke around when he would come downstairs from his room and say to him, whats up Malcolm X. It was all in fun and being a humorous type of person himself, he saw the comedic intent and took no offense.

He did have his serious side though and he showed it to me one day after me and Amanda got into a disagreement about some issues we were having in our relationship. Clark had taken his family over to one of his brothers house to visit. That particular day, it was about 106 degrees outside. Me and Amanda were arguing and things got really heated to the point of saying things that shouldn't have been said. Needless to say, Amanda stormed out of the house angrily and was presumably on her way across the street over to Clark's other brother house directly across from us. I locked the door on her with intent to keep her out until she calmed herself down. What she didn't know was that nobody was home at Clark's brother house. She stormed back to our house yelling and demanding that I open the door. I was determined in my logic that it was in my best interest to not open the door until she calmed herself down. She called Clark up and told him that I locked her out of the house but what she didn't tell him is why I did it. Knowing that it was scorching hot outside and being the type of compassionate man he is, Clark decided to come home to open the door and see if he could help bring some sort of peaceful resolve to the situation. Prior to his arrival however, Amanda decided to take matters into her own hands and kicked the front door open breaking the door casing from the wall.

When Clark arrived, even though I knew he had to

have been pissed off for having to drive all the way home to solve our dispute, he remained calm and promptly took Amanda off to the side in private to talk to her to hear her side of the story. Then he listened to my side and reminded me that Quran says that we are not to put our wives out of the house and we are not allowed to annoy them to the point they feel they must move out on their own. He told me that both me and Amanda were his guests and since she was his guest, he was the only person who had the power to tell her or anyone else in his house to leave. That is one of the things I appreciated most about this brother. He didn't take sides. He always tries to be fair and establish justice and if you are wrong on something, he was going to call you out on it. He didn't let our brotherly love for one another or our business relationship influence his assessment of how to handle the situation. He told me where I was wrong and told her where she was wrong and gave us an amicable solution by reminding us of what God says.

We had no choice but to submit because he was absolutely right and so me and Amanda smoothed things over and things got back to normal quickly. A few months passed by as we kept awaiting to hear from the attorneys about my case. Me and Amanda had talked about our living situation and although we were extremely grateful to Clark for letting us into his home, we kinda felt like it was time for us to try and get our own place. Initially we moved in with my sister Wendy but then we found an extended stay room which gave us our much needed privacy. By this time we had both landed jobs at a car dealership. She worked as one of the quality control clerks and I worked in auto detailing at that same facility. Now it is important that I note the fact that when we arrived in Atlanta, Amanda and I were just boyfriend and girlfriend.

Salih and Clark had suggested to us that we should protect our path to Allah by getting married. Knowing how much Amanda meant to me and after seeing how she stood by my side helping me, I didn't hesitate to make her my wife. We asked Salih to marry us. Clark and Malik acted as our Wali which means a witness. It was a modest wedding with just Salih, Clark, Malik, Hunter and Aaediin in attendance. Salih's wife and his sister Faye came over later and joined in our marital bliss bearing gifts for me and Amanda. Afterward, me and Amanda took a short trip for our honeymoon. We went to Kansas City.

My sister Janice had come to Georgia to visit. My sister was very over protective and screened every woman I took interest in. Janice had met Amanda when I was living in Flint when I first got released from prison. She really didn't like Amanda and basically gave her the cold shoulder right from the beginning. She accused her of wanting to be with me strictly for the possibility of money from my lawsuit. Even though she didn't like Amanda, things stayed quiet until one particular night. One night I heard her and Amanda arguing . My sister was calling her gold digging bitch and other things. Next thing I know, they began fighting like cats and dogs. Amanda got the upper hand over my sister and was on top of her hitting her. I pulled her off of her and told her we have to leave. I said go get your stuff now. She asked me to take her back over to Clark's house and so she went to get her belongings.

My sister had gotten up from the ground and left at that point. Amanda had brought some of her things to the car. I was just about to get into the car and then she rushed toward Amanda and once again, Amanda got the upper hand over her and had her pinned to the ground hitting her. She had thrown so many blows to my sisters face that it was red with blood and puffed up with swelling. I kept trying to pull her off. Finally I maneuvered my body in position to intercept her arms as she was barreling down to swing again. I pulled her off and stood in between them. My sister walked away saying with an emphatic tone, "this ain't over". We didn't see her anymore for about 15-20 minutes. During that time me and Amanda continued to load all of our stuff into the car so we could get ready to go back over to Clark's house.

Finally, we were ready to leave. I was getting into the car from the driver side as Amanda was entering from the passenger side. At that point I heard one of my nieces saying, what are you doing with that knife. Suddenly, my sister came rushing toward Amanda with a knife and this time it was a bigger knife. It was the big butcher knife kind. She had two of them and began swinging at Amanda. I immediately rushed over to that side of the car to try to stop them. Amanda put her head down and rushed into my sister. At the same time, my sister was in mid swing with that knife coming toward Amanda's head and neck area. As fast as I could, I reached to put my arm in front of Amanda hoping to deflect the knife. Instead, the knife went straight into my hand severing arteries. With the knife still lodged inside of my hand, I still had to deflect the other knife as my sister was swinging it at Amanda while trying to get the other knife out of my hand.

She had actually struck Amanda in her chest nearly piercing her heart and she stabbed her in her back directly adjacent to her lungs. A few more inches and she would have punctured her lungs. Finally we were able to get my sister away from Amanda and my other sister Wendy told me that we need to get her to the hospital. We rushed straight to the hospital. Now since these were stab wounds, by law the hospital has to notify the police. They came and took statements from both of us.

After having studied so much law, I wisely knew not to say much to the police and so as a result, the only statement I gave to them was that we were attacked. I didn't give any names or any details as to what caused the attack even though they kept probing me for more information. I told them that is all I will say without an attorney present. Amanda on the other hand was scared. She did give more detailed statements and based on what she told them, and after having gone to the house to look at the house for evidence, they placed both me and Amanda under arrest and took us into custody. I was highly pissed off. They were trying to pin an attempted murder and an assault charge on me in addition to providing a false statement to the police. All I was doing was trying to protect my wife from being injured and now once again, I found myself in the same situation I was in when I went to prison for protecting my sister. Plus I thought about how bad this would look for my upcoming case with my lawsuit against the DOC and the state of Michigan.

I called Salih to alert him of my situation. Keep in mind that I had been studying law for over 20 years and so I was well versed in what motions I needed to file so that I could be able to force the prosecutor to show me what evidence they had against me. I also wisely knew not to allow bail to be posted. This would have given them jurisdiction which I refused to yield. Eventually, I ended up beating the case and easily I might add. I beat the case because I never said anything to them except that there was an attack which was a true statement so therefore, they had to drop the making a false statement out. My wounds were defensive wounds and Amanda told them that I was not the one who cut her so that charge couldn't stick.   Unfortunately for Amanda, she did receive probation for having made false statements to the police.

That whole ordeal was an eye opening experience for me. I met up with Clark and Salih shortly after my release from jail and they told me that it was time I start to take the situation more seriously more-so now than ever because so much was at stake and bad publicity could ruin my chances in my upcoming court case. They convinced me to start thinking about more than just myself and to look at the big picture. They suggested the possibility of hiring a body guard to stay with me around the clock until the trial to keep trouble away from me. We discussed how the State of Michigan could and probably would be made aware of my arrest and incarceration and would use it against me. We decided that it was in my best interest to start cleaning up my image and present myself in the best possible light. They told me to use my experiences in law and my whole prison experience to become an inspiration to others. They were right because I had that burning passion in me anyway. I always wanted to be that mentor trying to help keep other young men and women away from trouble.

Shortly after all of that drama that happened between Amanda and my sister, I met a brother at a speaking engagement in Atlanta. He told me that he was fighting a case in Alabama for attempted murder. He was in Atlanta because the state of Alabama was allowing him to seek employment outside of Alabama pending his trial. He had been out on bond for 2 years. He was facing attempted murder charges against his girlfriend. He explained to me that it was merely domestic violence assault but the prosecutor was seeking attempted murder charges. This was his first encounter with the law and yet they were trying to give him 20 years in prison for the charges against him. Throughout my time in prison, I had met so many men who had similar cases. This ridiculous type of heavy sentencing was the norm for low income communities. This young man had a court appointed attorney who was trying to convince him to take the plea and accept the 20 years even though he didn't try to kill his girlfriend and even if he did, it was still a harsh sentence for a person who had never been in trouble with the law for any reason.

I offered to help him after having explained who I was. He could tell based on the legal strategies I told him that the attorney should have followed, that I knew what I was talking about so he gladly accepted my help. We made an appointment to meet with his attorney and so I drove all the way to Alabama. After meeting with this attorney, I determined that he didn't have this young man's best interest at heart. It was obvious. They had no evidence that he was trying to murder her and yet they were trying to offer him 20 years in prison. I asked the young brother to fire his attorney. He was able to pool enough money together to hire another attorney. We found this attorney through the American bar association. He was from Tuscaloosa, Alabama. We drove there to meet up with him. I explained to him that I was a paralegal and that I would be working closely with him on the case. He agreed to the terms and took the case. He signed me on as co-council which meant that I could sit in the courtroom with the attorney.

Finally the time arrived to pick the jury for this trial and for the trial to be underway. The jury was picked early that morning and the trial started later on that same day. I had advised the attorney to submit a motion for insufficient evidence. The prosecution was so eager to bring bogus charges that they didn't make sure they had all of the elements needed to secure a conviction. Not only did they not have physical evidence, they were not able to establish intent which is a mandate in murder and attempted murder cases. This young man ended up being found not guilty.

After the trial, as we walked out of the courtroom, the attorney shook my hand and said it was a pleasure working with me and offered me a job in Alabama. I turned it down mainly because I was not interested in moving to Alabama but also because I wanted to be the silent fighter behind the scenes fighting to ensure justice for all people. Nonetheless, I was still grateful and honored that my skills caused that attorney to consider me for a job working with him in law. This fueled my desire to use my legal expertise to help others even greater. I was elated. I had finally put what I believed was my purpose into real life action. I needed that feeling. It came at the right time and I was ready to take on the daunted task of doing my part to help change the world.

I helped them win that case and they paid me a nice amount for my work. This brought such an awesome feeling to my spirit. I had finally begun to do what I was most passionate at and I was ready to take it to the next level. Me and Amanda went back to stay with my sister Wendy because Janice had gone back to Michigan. We were able to go back to our respective jobs. We pretty much maintained our jobs there until we finally got that long awaited call from the attorney. They needed me to come back up to Michigan to start getting prepped for my upcoming trial. The trial date hadn't been officially set though because the judge still wanted us to try and have another settlement hearing to see if we could come to some kind of mutual agreement. I needed to be there anyway so that I could prepare for the settlement hearing as well. We felt it was in our best interest to just head on back to Michigan and with everything that was going on with Amanda, it was perfect timing. We couldn't afford to get ourselves in any more legal situations.

So, I called up Clark and let him know my situation. He decided to take us early Friday morning because he worked night shift and had to work Thursday night. Me and Amanda grabbed everything we could fit into that little Toyota Corolla to take back to Michigan with us because we were not certain if we would return anytime soon. We hopped in that little car and let me tell you, it was filled to the gills. The trunk was so loaded that you could see our luggage bulging out of the top of the trunk. We were packed in that car like sardines. It was me, Amanda, Clark, and his sons Malik, Hunter and Aaediin all jammed in that little car for nearly10 hours. Before we hit the road however, we rode with him to work but he dropped us off at one of his friend's house up in the mountains named Joseph while he worked the night shift at his job. We spent the night there until he got off from work early Friday morning. For that brief night we actually had fun even though we had limited phone service since we were up in the mountains.

Joseph treated us with great hospitality. The boys loved his dog. It was a big, huge tan colored bull dog. I think that dog kinda had a crush on my woman because he kept wanting to cuddle up with her. I thought it was cute at first but then I was like, lookie here Judge, (his name was Judge). I was like, you got to find yourself someone else to cuddle up with because this one is already taken. Judge just looked at me as if to say," unless you about to do something about it, then shut it up because I'm about to lay my ass right here." Judge was lucky I liked him too because otherwise, it was about to be on and popping. Finally Clark got off work and it was time to hit the road. We loaded up the rest of our stuff as if we were the Beverly Hillbillies and hopped onto the highway headed north instead of heading for Hollywood. It took us about 9/1/2 hours even though we stopped several times but finally we had made it back to Michigan.

Things looked slightly different because at that time, the streets were all being torn up to fix the underground water system because the pipes were lined with led. We basically went back to Flint during that Water Crisis which at this very moment while I am writing this book, is still ongoing. They still have not fixed the water problem. Needless to say, I was happy to finally be back home with all of those familiar family faces and especially mama's. I couldn't wait to see her again and as soon as that car stopped, the first thing on my mind was I wanted to go get mama. She hadn't met Clark and the boys yet so naturally she was eager to meet them since she had heard so much about them. It was a beautiful sight to see as she gave all three of them a warm long heart felt embrace that was mutually reciprocated.

Mama called Ralph over to meet Clark finally. The crazy thing is that although Ralph is my brother, he is Clark's cousin and they had never met before. When they say its a small world, that experience definitely proves that it is indeed a small small world. Clark wasn't able to stay long because it was Friday morning. He wanted to stop by to see his other family members and then get some rest for a few hours because he had to head right back to Georgia because he had to work on Sunday.

They came back over to say goodbye that next morning right before they were about to hit the highway headed back to Georgia. I thanked Clark for everything they had done for me and Amanda and mama gave him a big hug and thanked him as well. After they left I immediately began to map out my strategies for my next moves to help jump-start my newly chosen career as a motivational speaker. I started doing research online trying to find out exactly what I needed to do. I started doing a lot of social media networking in particular on Facebook. There we many people in my social network who knew of someone who had a level of expertise which could help me in my endeavor. As I met more people who could help, my excitement and zeal continued to increase. It reached a point where you could say I was a bit overzealous. I think maybe it was because I wanted this so bad. I needed to help my fellow inmates who saw no hope or who were questioning their faith. I needed to restore that in them and so I was eager to get this show on the road so I could make a difference.

Chapter 11
When Justice Became My Enemy

Finally the trial date was set after they had spent 6 years of legal maneuvering trying to suppress evidence, delay a trial or get the case thrown out altogether. The judged opened court by allowing oral arguments before the trial actually began. They filed a motion to dismiss the case. I have actual audio tape of one of the 3 Federal judges hearing my case responding to the defendants by saying and I quote, "What was Mr. Moore to do? He did everything in his power to submit documentation. This led me to believe they understood the basis of my lawsuit which was that I felt I was in danger and was not being protected.

Now it is important to note that back in 2012 when I had first filed my case against them, the judge ordered all parties involved in the case to turn over all evidence that was going to be used in the trial. Both parties did so presumably. They however, did not include any of the color photos of my injuries which we specifically requested or any surveillance videos that were their property but which we tried to subpoena into court as evidence. I had attorney friends who had written certified letters to the DOC which clearly stated that I felt my life was in danger and needed protection. These letters were in their possession which they did not turn over to the court as evidence. There were well over 100 plus documents which proved I felt I was in danger which they withheld. They asked for a dismissal of the charges. Thankfully the documents eventually were handed over to the court and I felt confident at that point that we had them where we wanted them.

Now throughout the whole time as my attorneys were preparing for my case, they had been allowing me to assist them because of my para legal background. They understood that I didn't want to leave no stone unturned and so I wanted to have a direct hands on approach to every aspect of my case. They obliged with exception to filing briefs. They were the only ones who prepared and filed all briefs that went before the courts. They told me they were impressed with my knowledge of the law and stated that they had never met a client who knew as much as I did. I understood all of the legalese language that attorneys use and so I was able to articulate myself and understand them as well. They even allowed me to give my opinions concerning what strategies we should use. They would bring stratagem and would listen to mine and weigh in and decide the best route to take. They seemed to have a passion for fighting against the DOC and I had over 20 years of experience as a para legal so it definitely seemed like a match made in heaven. We felt confident we could definitely win this case.

It should also be noted that on the eve of the trial, they filed a motion to suppress the evidence of letters sent by attorneys which were sent by certified mail and the receipts proving they did in fact receive those letters. The judge granted them their motion thus denying the jury the opportunity of viewing critical evidence. The judge also allowed them to enter into as evidence, documents that had not been previously turned over to me and my team during the discovery hearings. I started feeling as if the judge had somehow been possibly bought off but I still wanted to believe that justice would prevail in the end. Keep in mind that throughout the 6 years prior to trial , the judge had been ruling in my favor on practically everything. Now all of a sudden this same judge was doing everything within his power to undermine me and cause me to lose this case.

You have to understand the magnitude of what I was trying to do with my case. I was trying to impact the entire system by exposing the corruption in the penal system hoping my case would end up in the law books as a victory for the prisoners to be used in court should they ever find themselves in the same predicament. I was furious as I watched this judge rule against me on every important issue that would prove my case beyond any doubt. This judge turned on me and in doing so, my mistrust in a corrupt system was verified. I mean, I had all of the required evidence necessary to win a conviction and yet none of those 8 people in the jury box was going to see or hear any of it.

I can honestly say right now that the title Clark came up with for my book was nothing short of brilliant and even more prophetic than he could have imagined because as that judge began to turn on me and constantly do everything in his power to help them, justice had indeed become my enemy. With him being fair, and impartial they could not possibly win the case at all whatsoever period. Instead, he became their advocate and my adversary and I just couldn't understand why he would do such an evil thing against me when he presented himself for 6 years as an honorable man who had principles and values and what I thought was a commitment to upholding these so that his reputation and justice remain preserved and protected.

I had documents from the Michigan state Police clearly stating my claims against the DOC needed to be investigated, but yet the judge wouldn't allow it into evidence. I had statements from my brother Ralph and the Flint police department stating that my claims needed to be investigated but yet, the judge wouldn't allow it into evidence and so these were never seen by the jury. How is that justice? I really need to understand how can we as a people turn to the Justice department for justice when they have become our enemy? The DOC was already corrupt and then the judge presiding over my trial seemingly had become corrupt too? Furiously enraged does not adequately explain my emotions that day.

For 6 long stressful years as I waited patiently for my day in court, this same judge scolded the DOC for what they did to me. During that same 6 years, this same judge repeatedly scolded them for playing games trying to delay the trial indefinitely and I have transcripts and audio files to prove it, but yet, during the trial he turned against me and kept ruling in their favor. I kept asking myself throughout the trial, how much did they buy this judge off for or what do they have against him that they are using to blackmail him with? I can say this much in retrospect, I trusted him and the system and put my faith in them and they both failed me. The judge and the system became my enemy and there was nothing I could do about it and had no one to turn to.

Sadly, what happened to me can happen to any one of us so none of us should be so naive to think otherwise. I really think this judge had to have been bought off or threatened or something. I can't prove it but his actions obviously suggest something happened which caused him to change. I'll probably never ever know for sure why he turned on me and so I guess all I can ever hope for then is Justice from God because their kind of justice became and always will be my enemy. When the trial was over I went home unsure but yet hopeful that I would win a conviction. I knew my story had to have some impact on at least one or two members of that jury so I remained optimistic. Finally I got the news that a verdict had been reached. What was told to me was the worst news I had heard since I had been released from prison. Not guilty on all counts? What? Are they serious? This can't be right.

There is no way a sane and rational human being can hear my story and think for one second that the DOC did all they could do to protect me. Who was responsible for the arsenic poisoning I suffered? Was that my imagination? My medical reports proved I was poisoned. I was in solitary confinement so therefore, my food and everything was controlled by the higher ups within the system. Somebody on the outside had access to arsenic because no prisoner could have pulled that off without outside assistance. What about the fact they sent me back to the same prison with the inmate who stabbed me? I proved that the Federal law states that I must be separated from that inmate and therefore automatically protected even if I don't request it. How is sending me back to that prison not tantamount to a direct Federal violation and essentially a failure to protect just as I was accusing them of?

You can rest assured, I filed for an appeal and at the time of the writing of this book, I have not had my second chance in court on this matter. As I look back at all of this, I do sincerely regret what happened to Mr. Wellington. I didn't cause his death but I did try to cover it up and I am so so sorry for that and hope he is blessed with paradise God willing. I had to uphold a street code because I believed in that code and I knew that if I violated that code, my life would have been on the line so I did what I did. I can't take back what happened or bring Mr. Wellington back but I certainly wish it never happened. I paid the price for trying to cover up that murder by serving 27 years in prison. That was an extremely harsh penalty but I paid my debt to society like a man and with great regret and remorse. I was never a bad person before all of this happened and I proved throughout my 27 years in prison that I was and still am a good person.

I didn't deserve what happened to me while in prison. I was serving my time for my part in what happened to Mr. Wellington that night but I certainly didn't deserve to have so many attempts on my life for speaking out against the wrong that the DOC was allowing to happen within the prison system. I was merely trying to get justice for the prisoners and in retaliation, they tried to kill me even after I had so courageously saved the life of one of their own correction officers. They wanted me silenced. They wanted me dead for having the audacity to come against them and the establishment and powers that be. They were unsuccessful because I survived but to be honest, in a way, they were successful. They killed my faith in the justice system to the point that I recognize that they will do what they want to do in court no matter how much evidence you bring.

I never want anyone to feel sorry for me though for what I endured in prison all of those years because I made it out alive. Yes, they tried to break me but they didn't make me so they most certainly could not break me. I called upon God and He heard my calls and answered me. I am a free man because God made that happen. Nothing short of a miracle could have saved me from all of those stabbings. I am alive because that miracle came from God. Nothing short of a miracle could have gotten me released. I am free because of Divine Intervention from God. I firmly believe that either God or one of His angels told me to get up and go to the window that night knowing there was a pencil on the ground and that a porter was sweeping the floor right at that very moment. Either God or one of His angels told me what legal cases to write down on that paper that night while I was in solitary confinement which helped me get out. God was with me the whole time watching over me. I don't get into religious debate with nobody but I can say this much, can't nobody ever convince me that there is no God because I know for sure He is as real to me as real can get. He showed up when I needed Him the most.

Will I ever get true justice? That remains to be seen. I do know this much however, I can't put my faith solely in the system anymore. I turned to them for justice and they failed to deliver. I have learned now that I must always put my faith in God. He was the one who protected me and kept me alive. He was the one who helped me get out of prison when it seemed as if I was going to spend the rest of my life in that awful world. He is the one who I turn to as I heal from the trauma I went through as I laid on the floor bleeding with my neck sliced open. He is the one who I turn to as I look in the mirror and see my ear and neck scars. He gives me the strength I need as I fight back the tears each time I see in that mirror how they sliced my ear and cut my throat open and deliberately left me there to die. I have to live with that pain constantly and only God can take that burden away from my heart I carry with me each and every day.

God is the one who helps me get through all of the pain I experience when my head is pounding as a result of my eye being gouged out and placed in a cup by that heroic nurse. He is the one who sent her to me to save my life. He is the one who helps me find peace when I am trapped in the jungle of despair, pain, and what appears to be loss of hope and defeat at the hands of my enemies. If I never get justice in this life against those who tried to kill me and cover it up, I will still be ok. I am alive. Do you hear what I am telling you? I am alive. I got my justice. They tried to kill me and God was not having it. I won. That is the most important victory. I won. I made it out. God showed up and showed out. Justice had become my enemy and I can honestly say I am alive, I am free and I continue to live and prosper because when justice became my enemy, divine intervention is what saved me and delivered me. I am forever grateful.

Through social media networking, I teamed up with a beautifully spirited person named Diane. She became instrumental in helping me get in contact with some of the right people who had power and influence which could get me into many speaking engagements. Her enthusiasm and belief in my cause was all I needed to hear and I was eager to get the ball rolling. She along with Amanda, Clark, Taqualim and Salih became intricate players in helping make my book a reality. They helped mold and shape me into what I needed to become.

With their help, I became a voice for those who have no voice. I will continue to be an inspiration to others. I have dedicated my life to going to the prisons as a motivational speaker trying to help guide those women and men to a better path. I believe this is what God kept me alive for. I show Him my gratitude by being in service to Him. They tried to break me since I have been a free man. They offered my wife a plea bargain after that stabbing I tried to protect her from and yet they tried to give me 20 years to life in prison. I used my wisdom and legal expertise and single handily got all charges against me dropped. We sat in a jail for 28 days and on the second day they tried to pin 20 years to life on me after I had just served 27 years of my life in prison. They tried to bait me and my wife into accepting a 50 thousand dollar bond. My legal expertise assured me not to accept anything from them. I was not going to make the same mistakes I made in that murder case that sent me to prison for 27 years of my life.

I'm reliving that situation to help you understand what I have learned and how I will use it to help others. You see, my wife was white and they offered her 10 years of prison. Yes, they were trying to make an example of me. I had a court appointed lawyer who said he didn't know what to do to get me out of that situation. I told him these exact words: If you listen to me, me and my wife will walk out this courtroom and I promise you that. I told him to file an insufficient evidence motion.

As I have studied law, I learned that this particular motion is one of the most powerful and effective motions you can enter into court record for immediate ruling to either vindicate or force the prosecution to show their hand pertaining to what evidences and strategies they plan to use. It is the governments obligation to prove a case beyond any reasonable doubt. It is their obligation to seek justice and not necessarily just a conviction even if it means that they have to dismiss a case in the interest of justice which may favor the accused. In my case, the attorney did in fact listen to me and filed that motion and so did my wife's court appointed attorney. I defeated them and I am free.

As I reflect back on everything I have been through, I can honestly say that what I went through has indeed made me a better man. Life had thrown so much at me over that 27 year span of time in prison and I wouldn't wish that experience on nobody. Even after my life in prison, I stumbled along the way but yet I am still learning and still remaining appreciative of the gift of life. I had asked Allah "why me" so many times while I was going through what I went through. The answer to that question was always with me but I finally understood it when I became certain that I wanted to become a motivational speaker. That answer was, "why not you." I was being prepared for that very mission: to be a motivational speaker.

Each of these experiences became learning experiences which I definitely plan to use when I go to speaking engagements in the prison system. Much of what I went through are common occurrences with inmates throughout the prison system. The most important lesson I learned first and foremost is to always, always keep God first in all facets of my life. That is the single most important factor which helped me through everything I endured. When I get the opportunity to fulfill my dreams and travel from prison to prison teaching the prisoners how to deal with their respective situations, I will always stress that one point regardless of what religion they believe in. Keep God first. Always keep God first.

The second most important thing I would encourage them to do is to take a long look at themselves and evaluate who they are and who they want God to see them as in the hereafter. This is important because once you take ownership of who you are, you then have to make a critical decision. You have to decide whether or not you like what you see or not and then make a decision to change that perception. I would teach them that you always want to change yourself for the better but definitely be analytical of yourself so that you are always presenting the best of you that you can offer. It's not always about how tough you are in prison. Sometimes wisdom comes in knowing when to and when not to be a specific type of person. You don't always have to show your strength because sometimes and in fact most of the time, the prison population already knows who you are and what you stand for.

I will make sure I help those men and women understand that they have to think not only about their own selves but that they have to start thinking about their families because their families are indeed affected by their decisions and their incarceration. Mama stayed stressed worried about my safety every time she left that prison after a visit. I knew that she wished she could take me home with her and not being able to do so impacted her for that whole 27 years. She had to work extra harder at her job just to make enough money to have extra money to send to me so I could live a little bit more comfortable in prison. Just like mama, so many other family members made sacrifices and suffered financial strain all because I made decisions which caused me to be in prison. Therefore, my message to prisoners is to think about the whole family portrait and not just you in the picture when making decisions in your life. Every person in that family portrait will be impacted by your decision to steal, kill, cheat on your spouse, intoxicate your body or do something that would cause you to go to prison. I would tell them that they can rest assured that someone in the their circle of family and friends is going to be stressed out of their mind over them. I want them to always remember that this life we live in is not always about them.

One of my most happiest yet worst pains throughout my time in prison was watching other prisoners going home. I was happy they were going home but wished it was me going home instead. I had gained so many friends and had to say goodbye to them as they were leaving that awful place while wishing they could take me with them. It was a devastating feeling knowing I was being left behind. Wishing that it was me going home was enough to drive any man insane. I tried to rejoice for them but I wanted desperately for that to be me.

As I am nearing the ending of telling you this miraculous story of my life, I reflect back on one particular day in my life which I shared with you earlier which became part of the fuel and motivation that led me to this very day. You wouldn't be reading this book today had it not been for that one particular day in my life that means so much to my story. Recall that I told you all about how I had just watched the news and saw the triumphant release of Nelson Mandela from prison. It gave me a sense of hope that someday I too would walk out of those prison walls a free man. When that Caucasian prison guard called out my name saying, "hey Moore you wish that was you don't you? Don't get your hopes of because you're going to spend the rest of your life in here." I said to him with an emphatic assurance, man I ain't spending the rest of my life here. I'm going home someday I promise you that. That was back in 1991.

On January 18, 2012, I walked out of those prison doors finally after 27 years, a free man just like Nelson Mandela and just as I had told that arrogant prison guard that someday I would. Now tell me God ain't all powerful, all knowing, almighty and most merciful. I'm so humbled and grateful that I am a free man and just as it was for Nelson Mandela, my experiences can be a hope and inspiration to many others. When faced with similar situations, it is my hope and prayer that people can draw from me an empowerment that becomes their fuel of hope. I survived those stabbings for a higher purpose.

They tried to cut my ear off but I can still hear the call of God calling me to this mission to help my fellow man. They tried to cut my eye out but I can still see with clear vision what I must do to help be a motivation and mentor to young men and women to keep them out of the prison system. They tried to slice my throat but my neck is still firm and it is what keeps my head held high as I look into the heavens thanking my Lord for protecting me and delivering me from the clutches of

178

wicked people who wanted me dead and for what? For wanting justice?

Am I bitter about what happened to me? No. What I am is grateful. I cannot stress that point enough to you. I am grateful to God. This experience drew me ever more closer to God. I am a living proof and testimony that God hears prayers, intervenes and has power over all things. I never accepted prison as my home. I believed I would come home one day and here I am a free man telling you my triumphant story. The single most important thing I want you to learn from and be inspired by my experience is that I kept my faith in God and I put Him first. I never wavered in my belief in God. I talked to Him everyday in prayer and as a Muslim, 5 times a day to be exact. Throughout the years before my release, I constantly kept telling people that someday I would be free and I would use my freedom to be a motivation for others. I never wavered in believing my destiny was to be a beacon of hope. I believe God kept me alive for this moment in time.

I spent all of my 20's and 30's and most of my 40's behind prison walls. Many of those men became my family and although I do not miss prison life for one second, I do miss some of those who I left behind. I will never ever forget them and in particular the ones who helped me and looked out for me. Prison became one of my teachers of life and I hold the lessons and experiences and my comrades left behind so dear to my heart. I walked into that prison a young man barely 19 years old and afraid of the unknown. In 2012 after serving 27 years behind bars, I walked out of that prison more than just a free man. I walked through those prison doors triumphantly as a servant of God and as a helper and beacon of hope for my fellow man. I wish I had the power to save every person on earth but since that is not possible, I have dedicated my life to doing my part to save humanity one mind at a time. I am alive for this purpose and I intend to spend the rest of my life fighting in God's cause by becoming a

179

motivational speaker and using my legal knowledge and my prison experiences as a proof to the world that even when Justice became my enemy, even when they kept denying me parole, even when they tried to take my life, God witnesses all things and has power over all things and no force in existence can contend with Him.

In closing I say to each and every last one of you, no matter what life throws at you, NEVER SURRENDER, NEVER GIVE UP! You and God are more powerful than any obstacle life can throw at you. Why do I say you and God are more powerful? The most powerful thing you can do whenever any trial or tribulation is inflicted upon your soul, is to CALL ON ALLAH and WATCH HIM SHOW UP AND SHOW OUT. Even if He does His work through you, rest assured He has power over all things. I am so honored you took the time to read my story and I pray that from it, you become a better person. Let my life be a testimony for you and a beacon of hope to God's glory. I survived. Yes, that's right. I won! I am still alive, I am free and I am home. I am Maurice Moore and this was my story. All Praises be to God.

Maurice Moore and Clark Triplett

would like to

thank you for purchasing this book.

May our Lord continue to bless you and guide you in His
straight path.

Made in the USA
Monee, IL
04 May 2022